Adventures of
Charlie Thatcher

The Cloud Catcher

Gordon James Cook

Copyright © 2023 Gordon James Cook

All rights reserved.

No part of this publication may be reproduced, distributed, or transmitted in any form or by any means, including photocopying, recording, or other electronic or mechanical methods, without the prior written permission of the publisher, except as permitted by U.S. copyright law. For permission requests, contact: gordon_cook1@yahoo.co.uk

The story, all names, characters, and incidents portrayed in this production are fictitious. No identification with actual persons (living or deceased), places, buildings, and products are intended or should be inferred.

Cover Design by: Lizbe Coetzee

1st Edition, 2023

ISBN: 979-8-38-873947-6

Contents

Prologue - Fantasy 1
   Charlie's House 4
Chapter 1 - Reality 13
Chapter 2 - Dreaming 23
Chapter 2.1 - Commerce 27
Chapter 2.2 - Religion 39
Chapter 2.3 - Politics 53
   Dragons & Monkeys I 60
Chapter 2.4 - Virtue 71
   Dragons & Monkeys II 79
Chapter 3 - Awakening 95
Chapter 4 - Rising 107
Chapter 5 - Seeing 115
   High Society 124
Chapter 6 - Fearing 137
   Charlie The Thundercloud 147
Chapter 7 - Suffering 161
Chapter 8 - Releasing 173
   Blowing Out the Flame 178
Chapter 9 - Falling 181
Chapter 10 - Ending 185
   Charlie's Final Act 189
Epilogue - Forgotten 191
Epilogue 2 - Remembered 199

In Memory of

Tanya Colella
1976 - 2020

Prologue
Fantasy

'Fantasy is hardly an escape from reality. It's a way of understanding it' Lloyd Alexander

We start our story on a high, high up in the sky. High above the clouds, high above the aeroplanes. High above all the troubles and the strife of our modern world. One might suggest you imagine yourself to be a bird, though that would never do for the intro that has been planned. No, instead simply relax, tune in and allow yourself to use your mind's eye. The eye that can go anywhere, see everywhere, at any time, past or present, whenever it so chooses and whenever it is so allowed.

So above the clouds are we, suspended in the pale blue sea, where the sun never fails to shine, yet curiously it is never warm. Down below the day in question is itself indeed a chilly one. It is a clear December day. Cold and crisp, stark but beautiful.

Now, it has been suggested we are above the clouds, though that is not totally true. Today there are no clouds, only the imagining of clouds, as a few light wispy white trails meander lazily through the void.

Normally one would encourage you to stay here a while and soak it all in. Spend a little time watching the world go by below. Reset and gain a little perspective on things. Today though we have someone that is waiting for you. Charlie is down below, and he is waiting for you so that his story might begin. It is alas to this end then that we must now begin our descent.

Take a deep breath then, all the way into the bottom of the lungs.

Hold it.

Hold it.

Hooold it...

Okay, now let it go. Let it all go and relax.

Gently now you float down through the sky, gently toward the lands below. You could assume you know a little about which lands they are, though that is of little consequence and besides, I am already sure that you will recognise them. As you sink closer the mass of green gives way and the streets, and the houses all break into view.

Eventually your focus falls onto one particular street. A long street, with old houses, that all appear to have been constructed too close to each other. Yet there is ample space to the front and to the rear so that those who reside may step out for a little air, should they so wish. They rarely do.

A typical Victorian terrace street, though with fewer parked cars than you have come to expect. In the summertime you may still get to witness children playing here. Enlivened in their natural environment, with little fear and no constraints of self-consciousness. Today the roofs glisten with a lingering frost and smoke can be seen rising from an array of mismatched chimney pots.

Now your focus zooms into one particular house. A beautiful old two-story mid-terrace. Victorian red brick, proud bright chimney, recently laid tiled roof. A smaller space to the front but tendered with love. A mature magnolia rests naked and exposed against the winter chill. Several empty pots, cleaned, stacked, and slightly frosted, awaiting the warmth to return and usher them into their next spring.

Looking into one of the sparkling, freshly painted, white wooden sash windows, we get our first glimpse of a man. This man's name is Charlie. Charlie is currently dancing, in an old fashion, hand in hand, arm around waist, with a beautiful woman. That woman's name is Ebony. Ebony and Charlie are wife and husband. They have been wife and husband for quite some time. They have been very happy through almost all of it.

Come on, let's go in and get a closer look.

Charlie's House

There is a bricked porch area to the front door. A beautiful old wooden Victorian door freshly painted a deep dark green. On the door hangs a naturally stayed wreath. It is December of course. It is the season for wreaths. The floor in the porch has been tiled. The tiles are small and coloured with oranges, blues, whites, and a dash of yellow. We enter the house, and find ourselves standing on spotless wooden floors, stained dark. It is cold outside, but it is truly warm here. There is a stairway directly ahead of us and we are immediately hit with a scent of warm, cinnamon, cleanliness, and winter bloom.

To our left is the living room and here we can again see Charlie. He is an older gentleman, though standing there, looking as grand as he does, you would struggle to state, exactly, of how many years. Today is a Saturday and it is the afternoon.

Charlie appears dapper as always. He is dressed in a smart two piece fitted wool suit. The suit is sky blue in colour and beneath the jacket he is wearing a crisp white cotton shirt, top button undone. Normally you might find Charlie wearing a tie, but today is Saturday and on the weekend, he opts for the more casual look. Today Charlie wears his favourite light brown brogues, looking out of the box fresh.

Currently within his embrace we find Ebony. Through Charlie's eyes, Ebony's almond shaped eyes sparkle like sunlight bouncing off water. Her skin exudes warmth, like the red sunrise that rises against clouds on a late winter morning, offering with it a tantalising promise of spring. Hair now silver, still worn to the shoulder, soft and silk like it shines. Lips, although not as full as they once were and now framed by lines of laughter, still invite and are still soft to the touch. Standing of roughly equal height Ebony wears an elegant cotton sheath dress, cut just below the knee, also sky blue in colour, paired with a soft white cropped cardigan and modest indoor heels.

Looking at the pair together you could be forgiven for thinking they have dressed up for a night out. They are however content in each other's company and their efforts are for each other alone. A radio is playing in the background whilst Charlie and Ebony share a slow dance.

"I miss dancing." Stated Charlie.

"What do you mean you miss dancing? We are dancing now." Was Ebony's reply.

"No. I mean I miss real dancing. You know, when we were young and free, and my hips weren't sore from the effort of it."

"Oh, my Charlie, you have gotten old before your time haven't you."

The truth is that Charlie had always been more of a 'glass half empty' type. He tended to look at the world, and back into the past, through glasses that were a little smudged and slightly scratched, rather than tinted with rose. Ebony was always the one that brought the sunshine, whereas Charlie was more the master of rainy days.

The music is interrupted, as the radio programme announcer announces that it is time, once again, for the news.

"The News. Pah! Why do they think we need to hear the news every single hour of our lives?"

"I'm assuming that's a rhetorical question Charlie. I'm also assuming that you are about to tell me the answer too?"

"No need to be sarcastic." Replied with a smile in his voice. "The truth though is that they feed people this every single hour to keep people afraid. When people are afraid, they are easier to control. Most of the news is the same old stories, just going around and around and around, generation after generation after generation. They used to say people should be afraid of God. Now they make people afraid of losing their house, or of catching disease, or of being attacked and murdered in the local park. And it will be people's fault if they do ever get attacked and murdered, because we moaned about paying too much tax and so they couldn't afford enough police. And so, people get angry and shout about it and then the government uses the police, the very establishment that the people have paid for to protect them, to attack them, and make people afraid of them as well. And then people hate the police, instead of hating the people we paid to employ the police to protect the people, from the other scarier people in the world, that the news likes to tell everyone about, every single hour. I mean, we pay a licence and..."

Ebony, now sitting, stared into the middle distance, eyes slightly glazed, forehead frown free.

"...we don't even get a say in how they spend that licence. I mean, for example, whilst I might admire his integrity, how is it right to use our money to pay an already rich ex sports star such extortionate amounts of money, to present programmes about sport, that most of us are not really interested in. No one with any real sense anyway. I mean, sports, that's another thing. Why do I need to hear about sports every hour? I don't care. There's a lot of people interested in knitting in this world, but they don't talk about that every hour do they. And why is that? I'll tell you why. Because sports teach us to compete. Celebrate the winners and pity the losers. Instead..."

Ebony, now wearing a more thoughtful expression and stroking her chin with her left hand, was considering what they might eat for dinner that night.

"...of just getting along. Why can't we all win? There is enough on the planet for everyone, why can't we all just get along and share everything. The media offers us false idols. Idols that they can then ritually sacrifice on their media alter to keep people interested in their media junk. Usually when there is a bigger political story happening in the background that they would rather you didn't see..."

Fish and chips. Yes, it felt like a fish and chip dinner was in order and... Wait, was he still going on?

"Jesus Charlie, let it go. Not everything is a conspiracy you know."

Having been so rudely interrupted Charlie stood silent now, with his mouth slightly agape.

"Oh Charlie, you do like to live your life under a cloud don't you. You may have spent your whole life under a cloud. In fact, I think that maybe we ought to catch you a real cloud. One of your very own. We can attach it to a piece of silver string, you can tie it to your wrist, and then you can take it with you wherever you go. That way everybody who sees you will know, before they even speak to you, that there goes a gloomy man. A gloomy man living under his very own cloud."

Ebony finished the line with a smile bright enough to light the whole street and warm enough to banish any chill that the winter outside might have threatened to impose.

"I'm just a realist." Said Charlie in retort. "I'm not negative, just honest. I can't help it. I was born this way. Besides, not everyone can be as cheery as you. Just imagine how miserable that would be, if everyone in the world was as annoyingly happy and content as you are."

With that Charlie abandons his verbal tirade and offers to fetch drinks from the kitchen.

"Oh yes please Charlie, that would be lovely."

So, Charlie takes his leave from the living room and walks into the adjoining kitchen. Still talking with Ebony, Charlie reaches for the cupboard above the kettle, the one where their best glasses are stored. Charlie retrieves two crystal tumblers and sets these on the side. He makes his way to the fridge, opens the freezer section, and takes out the ice cube tray. He places a single cube of ice into each of the glasses then returns the tray to the freezer. Next, he pulls open the large drawer that sits underneath the stove. Here he locates a fresh bottle of single malt, reserved for special occasions, such as Saturdays. He smiles and pours a single neat measure into each glass. He then returns the bottle to the drawer and slides it closed. He picks up the glasses. Anticipation, the peaty smell of the spirit, the company he is in. All make his mouth water as he calls out to the next room. "I'm coming in with the drinks now."

There is no reply.

As Charlie approaches the threshold of the kitchen, he senses that something is not right. Something is in fact very wrong. The sun appears to have dipped below the horizon now and suddenly there is a deep chill in the air. All the colour in the room appears to have drained. A stale, dank damp smell begins to make itself known and the radio is starting to transition, from big band music into white noise. Everything begins to fade, and Charlie is now standing there in his living room, alone.

There is no radio playing.

The room is silent.

There is no sunshine coming in.

Charlie looks down and sees two glasses in his hands, both filthy, reeking of cheap whiskey.

He becomes aware of the tatty suit he is wearing.

Soiled, torn, stained, worn day in, day out.

He knows no different.

His shirt hangs out from the top of his trousers.

A soul, barely attached, flaps open at the front of his left shoe.

Eventually Charlie gathers the courage to look into the centre of the room, the empty room, and remember that there is no Ebony anymore. Ebony has gone.

Ebony died many moons ago.

Charlie lives alone.

Correction.

Charlie is alive, alone.

Ebony is gone and Charlie lives on.

Alone.

Reality

'Three things cannot be long hidden: the sun, the moon & the truth' Buddha

Once upon a time, on a clear and sunny winter day, the sky a crisp pale blue, there existed, underneath that sky, a street. The street was a normal street, much like the ones you and I live on or live near, and on this street, there was a house. One of many, the house was nothing special. It wasn't overly big, and it wasn't particularly small. In fact, it looked much the same as all the other houses on the street, except this one was now visibly tired and neglected.

The moss and frost covered roof supported several cracked tiles, in need of desperate repair. The chimney mortar needed replacing; water being allowed in the meantime to leak into the upstairs rooms. The garden to the front was messy, unloved, overgrown. A naked magnolia tree shivered amongst the debris dotted around of various broken, tired, and forgotten pots, housing nothing now but frosted mud and the skeletal remains of plants long since departed.

Children in the street never went near this house. Mostly one supposes because there was never any reason, for only one person lived in this house and he was not a child anymore, but a man. Not just a man, but an old man. Not just an old man, but a lonely old man.

The name of this man, this lonely old man, is Charlie Thatcher. At least that is what he remembers he is called. It had been a long time since he has heard anyone say his name. Still, that is the name that appears on the bills when they come. Charlie is happy for the bills. He is happy that his name is Charlie and that someone out there still wishes to communicate with him.

Charlie sits alone in that house today. He sits alone in that house every day. He has sat alone in that house every day now for many years. So many years he has lost count. The house consists of two floors. The tired front door opens to a tired wooden floor, now showing signs of rot, which leads to a carpeted staircase, threadbare and faded. On the left there is a living room. The living room leads into a diner then on into a kitchen, which then leads onto a toilet and bath at the back of the house. There is a door in the kitchen that opens onto a backyard. The space is thin but long. Too small for plants and socialising, this space has instead been deemed a worthy dumping ground and has by now amassed a good number of sodden black bags, their rotten innards leaking and combining to form a slippery sheen of slime across the cold dark stone surface.

Back through the living room a staircase can be found and ascended to the two bedrooms above, the master bedroom and a smaller, adjacent guest room. It seemed fraudulent to Charlie to name the latter as such, based on the fact it had not seen a single guest in all the years he had lived there. As for the master bedroom this was now a redundant area reserved exclusively for ghosts, spiders, and dust mites. Charlie had not climbed those stairs, nor set foot in the master bedroom, for at least twelve months now, choosing instead to spend his nights reclined and restless on the stale brown sofa that occupies the living room.

Living room. Here was another misused title. Charlie was alive all right, at least in the physical sense of the word. But living? Well... Throughout each day Charlie will sit in his worn-out armchair, one part of a two-piece suite, that may have been fashionable sometime in the seventies but would not appeal even to the retro markets of today. Brown in colour and patterned with lighter brown dots, fully cushioned on the seat and back and with padded arms. A single armchair paired with a three-seater sofa, though three people would never feel comfortable sitting that close together. Thankfully this was something Charlie didn't have to worry about as no one ever came to visit and the sofa, as has already been mentioned, was instead now used as Charlie's bed.

The space in the room was large but relatively empty, always feeling cold. South facing, it was a blessing in the afternoons, but the chill remained, nonetheless. A brown floor to ceiling curtain was hung over the front door to help block any drafts. The curtain however was worn and single skinned and sagged in places from the rail. In the living room was a bay window with a view onto the street. An obligatory net curtain, tinged yellow, held the stage here and ensured that whilst Charlie could see 'them', the 'them' could not see Charlie. In the same faded brown as the door curtain there hung two curtains here too, like tired, senile guards on sentry duty, standing between Charlie and the outside world.

Regarding the outside world, Charlie's was, these days, very small. Consisting of a Post Office and a few other shops located at the end of the street (a mini supermarket, a hardware store, a fish and chip shop). Charlie was forced to venture here at least once a week, to collect his pension and to stock up on microwave meals. To pay for his bills and milk deliveries and, once a week, put out for a large portion of chips and a fishcake. Whilst Charlie was a regular to these establishments nobody ever seemed to see him. Staff would acknowledge him of course, but nobody ever really looked at Charlie. Except maybe the young girl server at the chip shop. He remembered the first time he saw her, how nervous she seemed. He remembered how nervous he felt, having to deal with someone new. He put on his brave face though and gave her an encouraging smile that day. Now, it turns out, she is the only one to ever make any effort to make eye contact. They never shared any real words, but she would always make an effort to share a smile. This filled Charlie up more than the chips ever could.

Aside from the girl at the chip shop, Charlie hated going out into the world. It felt as if others were constantly staring at him. Looking at his unclean clothes, casting judgements, making assertions, based on his gait and unkempt appearance. Charlie would like to say he didn't care but he did. He wished he could be invisible on his trips out, wished he could hide himself from the sky and all the unkind thoughts that swim about within it. The outside world filled him with fear, and it would always take Charlie at least an hour to summon up the courage to even step out of the front door. Here in the house at least, whilst it may be cold and dark, Charlie felt safe. This feeling was the only valued feeling he had left.

The carpet from the living room extends out to a dining area and is a faded shade of green. In fact, teal may be a better description. Regardless of what colour you will call it, it is mostly faded and sticky and horrible. Tiny beetles like to gather and feast on the carpet edges. Not helping is the fact that this carpet has not locked horns with any type of suction device in well over five years. The broken hoover that resides under the stairs has never been replaced. By now the cumulative dust has added its own shade of grey to the carpet and now frames the walkways regularly shuffled along by a solitary Charlie. The dining area still has a table. It is rectangular, made of smoked glass, floated on gold metal chrome legs. With room for four there are four accompanying chairs, metal framed, ugly, hard, and uncomfortable. Charlie eats his dinners off his lap whilst sitting in his armchair.

Other items in the room include an old gas fire, yellowed from age. A tired looking pine television stand, topped with an old, heavy square, with buttons that need to be pushed to change the channel. This TV however is not plugged in, and the screen offers only a presentation of caked dust by way of entertainment.

There are no pictures on the wall anymore. Only the ghostly outlines remain to indicate where pictures might once have hung. Finding them too hurtful to look at, Charlie had long since taken them down and stored them under the stairs with the broken hoover. Only one picture remained. A small, wooden framed, black, white photograph of Ebony and Charlie, side by side, hand in hand. A picnic by the canal. A perfect day to be remembered. Ebony had left Charlie many years ago now. The picture was taken when they were both young, healthy, and with their whole lives ahead of them. This is how Charlie liked to remember Ebony, and this is the only remaining item in Charlie's world that he cares about. It is here, where Charlie focuses his attention every day. It is this picture that takes Charlie through the long endless emptiness of each day. In contrast to everything else in the room, no dust has been allowed to settle here.

Charlie, now sitting on the couch, stares at the picture, as he does every evening. He remembers Ebony's smile. He remembers Ebony's warmth, in spirit and in touch. He remembers Ebony's boundless positivity, even at the end. Ebony was the Ying to Charlie's yang. He yearned for her more with every passing day. He wished he could be more like her. He wished he could be with her.

'He was sick of this world, sick of consumerism, sick of religion, sick of politics. A world now seemingly devoid of good virtue and decency and...' Here Charlie stopped in his train of thought and smiled to himself

> *'Oh Charlie, you do like to live your life under a cloud don't you. You may have spent your whole life under a cloud. In fact, I think that maybe we ought to catch you a real cloud. One of your very own.'*

Remembering this now made Charlie smile. The thought of his very own cloud. Wouldn't that be a thing. He could hide himself underneath his cloud and never be exposed to the pain of the world again. Yes, to catch himself a cloud, Charlie thought, would be a very fine thing indeed.

It was with this thought in mind that Charlie closed his eyes. As he imagined life with a cloud, he slowly found peace. Sleep shortly followed.

Dreaming

*'The best way to make your
dreams come true Is to wake up'*
Paul Valery

"Psst. Charlie. Open your eyes. Open your eyes, Charlie."

Wait, he knew this voice, but it couldn't be. This was the voice of his wife Ebony, sounding as young as he remembered. Dare he? Dare he open his eyes?

Charlie opened his eyes.

He found himself led down. He was lying on a woollen blanket, green tartan in pattern, that had been laid out on the grass. Ebony was propped up on one elbow looking down upon him and gently stroking the bridge of his nose with the index finger from her free hand.

"There you are." She said gently.

Ebony was gazing down upon him. The warmth of her hand was now cradling the side of his face. Her hair was rich and dark and shone in the sunshine. Her face was smooth and full of the radiance of youth. Ebony was smiling, a full and beautiful smile that was just for him, and him alone.

Charlie looked into her eyes and smiled back. Then, with a jolt, Charlie sat upright. The first thing he noticed was how easy it was to sit upright and the lack of any pain. The second thing he noticed was the clarity of his senses, all having long since been dumbed down by the onset of age.

"What the... I mean where the... I mean, where am I? What is happening? What... What... How did I get here?" Then, in a slightly higher pitch, "where is here? I mean, am I... is this... you know... have I kicked th..."

"Charlie, Charlie, calm down will you. It's alright. Everything is alright, you are fine."

"Then what is this, what am I doing here?"

"We have come out to catch you a cloud silly billy. Remember?"

"But I... I was not here. I mean I was not here, but I was somewhere else. You, you left me, you were gone, and I was old and... And I... Forgive me, I don't understand."

"Breathe Charlie, breathe with me. It was just a dream. You were just dreaming. Take a deep breath and relax. You are fine. Everything is fine. Everything is okay now."

Ebony smiled at him and gently held his hand. This helped Charlie to calm down and he looked around to take in his surroundings. They were essentially led out in the middle of a grassed area, running alongside a canal and a canal path. Two white swans were traversing the waters, looking to catch the attention of people passing by that might have some seed upon their person. It was a sunny day; the skies were deep blue. The air was clean, and Charlie could feel the warmth of the sun, just right, upon his face.

"To catch a cloud, you say?" Questioned Charlie, now with a smile forming upon his face.

"Yes Charlie, to catch a cloud. To catch you a cloud. Today is the day that you finally get a cloud of your very own."

"Ha, amazing. But how do we go about finding a cloud to catch? It is such a beautiful day. I can't see any clouds anywhere."

"Well Charlie, we are going to take a wander in that direction." Ebony pointed to the Southeast. "There is a daily market there and I am sure they will have a cloud pen from which we can pay to catch one."

"Ah yes." Said Charlie, reverting now back to his good old cynical self. "Nothing quite like commerce and the free market. We are bound to find what we are looking for there. Everything we need apparently. And everything we didn't know we needed too. Especially in this day and age, where you can find everything anywhere and..." Charlie paused. "Where is this day and age by the way?"

Ebony simply smiled and nodded her head left to right. Standing up she reached down and took Charlie's hand. After pulling him up to his feet the couple moved off, Ebony leading the way and Charlie following.

Commerce

'The difficulty lies not so much in developing new Ideas as in escaping old ones' John Maynard Keynes

Ebony and Charlie crossed the short distance across the field upon which they had lain. At the edge of the field was an old, cobbled road, and on the other side of that road was a bustling marketplace. The site upon which the market took place was huge. Charlie saw this was predominantly a food market, though there were an equal number of stalls devoted to other wares, including books, electronica, art, trinkets and the like. The stalls were awash with life, hustling back and forth, browsing, bartering, laughing, arguing, eating, drinking, belching, farting, adjusting their trousers and scratching, looking, and thinking and being and being and being and being.

"We are here to see the Market Manager." Informed Ebony as she led Charlie into the thick of this human mass. Following Ebony's lead, they weaved their way through and in between the various stalls toward the centre of the marketplace. Once in the centre they happened upon a small building. A simple structure large enough to house a fair-sized single room.

The door to this building seemed a little over the top. Fashioned of reinforced steel, it looked more like the door of a safe than of an office. Unlike a safe though, the top half of this door held a window, albeit a window of mirrored glass, tinted a smoky colour, making it very difficult to see through. To the side of the door, fixed to the door frame, was a door knocker. This was silver and fashioned in the shape of a dollar sign.

"Classy." Remarked Ebony, whilst grabbing said dollar and using it to bash against the frame three times.

'Doof, doof, doof.'

After no more than a minute the door swung open. Standing proud within the doorway was the cutting figure of a beautiful and confident woman. The first thing Charlie realised was that he was surprised to see a woman standing there. He had assumed that the boss of the marketplace would be a man. The second thing Charlie realised was that he was a bit of a sexist. This was a depressing and sobering thought. A better thought was that, now enlightened, he might at least do somewhat better with his assumptions in the future. He resolved to do his best and to be less sexist going forward.

The woman in question was of average height, slim build, striking eyes and bright fire red hair. Wearing a look that told you she had seen it all before, she beckoned them both in and closed the door behind them, instantly drowning out the noise and the chaos of the marketplace.

"Bonjour."

'Damn it!' Thought Charlie to himself, having assumed she would be Irish.

"My name is Laissez-Faire and this... This, my bon amiss, is my marketplace. I welcome you both here with open arms. Now, without further ado, may I offer you both a drink? Absinthe per'aps?"

"Absinthe? Isn't that a little strong for this time of d... Ouch!"

Ebony, whilst retrieving her elbow from Charlie's ribs, replied. "Absinthe would do just fine. Thank you."

Laissez-Faire offered an approving smile then set about preparing the drinks. After handing drinks to Ebony and Charlie she waited until they both had taken a sip, then stated that these would cost five euro each. Charlie spluttered. Unhappy that he was now indebted, he protested that if he would have known there was a charge then he would not have accepted the drink. Laissez-Faire snorted, shrugged, then retorted, saying this was simply the way of the world. She then turned to Ebony and asked what it was that they were here looking for.

"Well Laisse-Faire, purveyor of fine goods and provider of overpriced beverages. We are in the market for a cloud."

"Pmph... A cloud you say?"

"Pmph yes, a cloud." Confirmed Charlie rather petulantly. "This is a marketplace is it not. Everyone knows that anyone can find anything they want in a modern market place these days. Supply and demand being king and all that. So yes, we are looking for one of your finest clouds if you would be so kind."

"Well, alas my friends, but we do not sell anything as exotic as a cloud. I am afraid that your faith in the free marketplace has been misplaced. We do not have what you currently desire."

"But... Ahem, well, you see... We came all this way. We can't go home without a cloud." Followed by, "...are you not able to order one in perhaps?"

"Ah, bon Ami, fear not. I am unable to order one in, but I do know of a place where clouds are made. Up on the Mountain side, not far from here."

"Oh. A cloud factory?"

"Hmmm. Non. No, not quite a factory. Actually, it is a church. It is said that the residing father there, a good man, is often hidden, he and his church, behind great clouds. I am sure he will be able to provide you with a cloud of your very own."

"Excellent!" Exclaimed Charlie. "In that case we should be off. Thank you for your ass..."

"But wait. You will of course require something to trade. The church is very rich already so you will need something other than money."

"Uh, okay. Well then, this is a marketplace. Do you have something you could suggest that we could offer the father in trade?"

"Oui, you are in luck my friends. I know of the father there very well, and it just so happens I have just the thing."

Laissez-Faire walked over to an old desk in the corner of the room, from which she procured an old, tattered looking deep rectangular box. She carried the box over and placed it on the desk in front of Ebony and Charlie. She then lifted the lid to reveal a small blue model train residing inside. Charlie felt somewhat disappointed by the revelation and felt it appropriate to say so.

"Ah." Replied Laissez-Faire. "You demonstrate only your lack of knowledge of such things. This is a very, very, very rare example. In fact, it is the last of its kind. The Father you go to speak with will take this in trade no question. The only concern here is whether you can afford it, no?"

Afford it. Charlie hadn't really considered money until now. It suddenly dawned on him that he had no cash about his person at all, and that they were already 10 euro in debt. It hadn't occurred to him that they might need to pay for something and this system all suddenly seemed most unfair.

Whilst Charlie was busy fretting in his head, Ebony stepped in and took over.

"You do realise that we are on a mission to catch a cloud." A rhetorical question. "Clouds are a natural phenomenon and so ultimately should cost nothing to acquire."

A laugh burst from Laissez-Faire. "Cost nothing to acquire!" She exclaimed. "Cost nothing to acquire!" Exclaimed again for good measure. "And just what do you think might happen to society if everything suddenly cost nothing to acquire? My whole empire is built on the very fact that everything, and I mean everything, has a value. Anyone who is willing can offer a service or sell their wares, and those that are good at it can make a pretty penny no."

"You mean those best suited to exploiting the system of course?"

"What do you mean? The system is fair. All have a fair chance. This is what Capitalism is, no? The chance for any individual to work hard and to accumulate capital, and then to sell or loan that capital at a price the market is willing to pay."

"It is a flawed system that not everyone gets the chance to exploit. There are those that could be successful but for lack of education, or for support, or for financial backing, or for having other responsibilities or for just being born as the wrong type or in the wrong place. There are people that just want to work hard and be fairly rewarded for the work that they do. Capitalism however values wealth over justice and equality, leading to the inevitable exploitation of those that just want to get by. For someone to be defined as rich, someone must first be oppressed and defined as poor. Wealthy people can only exist where there is poverty and it becomes in their interests to keep the poor poor, so that they can continue to enjoy the status and the benefits that their money brings."

"Don't be so naïve. Those poor that you refer to are just lazy, everyone knows that. Besides, we have welfare in place to take care of the less fortunate. I myself donate a sizable sum each month to the local food banks. Capitalism works and unless you can demonstrate to me as otherwise, you owe me 10 euro for the drinks and another 1,000 euro should you wish to acquire this train."

"1,000 euro! Are you kidding me? For a toy train!"

"The real question, madam, is how much is your cloud worth, no?"

Ebony was infuriated for a moment, then stopped and reflected on what had just been said.

"Wait. You said if I can demonstrate that capitalism is flawed you will wipe our debt and give us the train for free?"

"Well, this is not exactly what I said. I said th… "

"But seriously." Interrupted Ebony. "If I can give you an example, that capitalism has a fundamental flaw, you will, in return, allow us our drinks and that toy train for free?

"Ha ha ha… Okay then my silly English friend. If you can raise to the challenge, and give me a fair example, then this will be so." Laissez-Faire took a seat, then took a long swig of her absinthe, reclined back into the chair, then smiled at Ebony. "I wish you the best of luck."

"Right then, here goes."

Ebony Began.

"Let us pretend that this room is one of many. A reception room within a large and exclusive hotel."

"Okay."

"You can be the hotel owner and I; I will be a potential guest from out of town."

"Hmmm..."

"I arrive at your hotel. I put down a 10-euro deposit on the side, as part payment up front. I say I want a room but that I would very much like to inspect them first. You agree and let me upstairs to inspect the rooms."

"Okay."

"When I have gone you grab that money and dash out to use it to pay a debt that you owe, say, to the butcher, for supplying your restaurant with some sausages that morning. The butcher then visits the baker, in order to clear a 10-euro debt with them. The baker, as it turns out, bumped into Charlie in the marketplace and agreed to buy a lovely hat from Charlie. The baker had no cash at the time so took the hat on credit. Now the baker comes back here, to your hotel, to pay Charlie the money he owes. Charlie, of course, owes you 10 euro for the drinks, so he drops the money onto your counter."

"Okay. Where is this going?"

"Well, at this very same moment I come back down the stairs. I declare your hotel to be a disgusting cesspit, snatch my 10 euro back off the side and leave. The end result is that no-one now has any debts, but no-one now has made any money."

"I, err, wait. This can't be ri..."

"Capitalism's flaw is that it is built on the idea of the accumulation of wealth via trade. Money provides the symbolism to support this idea. Wealth, however, is not actually a real thing. Only the idea of wealth exists. You may have 10 million euros in a bank account somewhere. In reality though, you only ever have what you have to hand at the time. Wealth is an illusion, and capitalism is the wonderland that has been built on this illusion. At any given time, a person's money can be snatched away. No matter how hard they do, or do not work for it."

Laissez-Faire sat with a stunned, confused look upon her face. She knew this could not make sense but was at a loss right now as to how she could argue against it. How could it be that money could circulate so freely but, when the controller of that money snatched it away, nobody would have anything to show at the end of it all.

Charlie meanwhile knocked back the rest of his absinthe, smiled at Ebony, and picked up the box containing the toy train.

"It was a genuine pleasure to meet you Laissez-Faire." He said with a wave on his way out the door. "Your market is genuinely wonderful but maybe it's time for a rethink. Maybe it is time for another way? Thank you for the drink, and of course for the train."

And with that Charlie and Ebony left the building.

Laissez-Faire was of course several euros down, on the train and the drinks. But maybe the exchange had offered up something more valuable. Right now, though she couldn't think what that could be.

Religion

'Convictions are more dangerous foes of truth than lies' Friedrich Nietzsche

So onwards for our heroes. Onwards and upwards. Up the mountain they did climb. Their next destination, a sacred church. A hallowed place at which, apparently, clouds were made.

On route to the church, they happened upon a crossroads. Straight across and the mountain continued upwards. To either the left or to the right the land flattened out then went back downhill. One way to rise, three ways to fall. There was a post set by one of the roads, against which a man did lean. A man. A lean looking man. About

6.2, dressed sharp in an old fashioned 50's style pin stripe suit. Dark hair, short and slicked back with oil. A pencil thin moustache and rather thin eyebrows. The man was smoking a cigarette, housed in a cigarette holder. Charlie smiled and nodded in the man's direction. In return the man smiled back, tapped his cigarette, to drop its ash, and nodded back. For a moment Charlie thought he saw the man's eyes glow, then thought maybe not. They continued past and carried on their way up the mountain and toward the church.

The church itself was a modest affair, set back from the road but visible to any who passed by. Charlie and Ebony entered the church grounds by a small iron gate and made their way up the path toward the main entrance.

The church door was of a typical design for a church. Old dark oak, arched at the top and split into two halves. Ornately decorated with wrought iron but with no window to look into. About a third of the way up, on the half to the right, was the door knocker. This was made of gold and fashioned in the style of a cross.

"Tasteful." Remarked Ebony, whilst grabbing said cross and using it to bash against the door three times.

'Doof, doof, doof.'

After about a minute Ebony repeated the process.

'Doof, doof, doof.'

After a third time it became clear to them both that nobody was home. Choosing then to explore the outside they eventually happened upon the Father in the church graveyard. The Father was not a tall man. Tubby might be the best word to describe his physique. Bald on top, grey elsewhere he might be said to resemble a monk, were it not for the full-bodied moustache and obligatory dog collar he chose to wear. He was busying himself with his creation of what appeared to be a rather elaborate train set. Tracks were set both here and there and weaved many routes amongst the aged and forgotten stones. Upon approaching the father, Ebony couldn't help but question out loud as to whether the laying of these tracks might be regarded as a little disrespectful?

"Pah..." Was the father's response. "The people here have long since gone back to the Earth. There are no relatives left to visit them and I can very much guarantee that the residents themselves don't mind a dot. In fact, I often like to think that my train tracks here are providing them with some form of entertainment. Eternity can be a very long time you know, and it's always good to have something to break up the monotony, don't you think? Besides, the local kids love it, and if it makes them happy then I too am happy. And as it is the kids that are alive now, then they take precedence over these old has-beens."

"Fair enough." Ebony conceded.

"Anyway." Said the father, "Please excuse my manners. I am Father Thomas McKenzie, and this is my church. Very pleased to make your acquaintance. What brings you my way may I ask, and how may I be of assistance?"

The father is clearly a good man, thought Charlie.

"Well, my name is Charlie, and this is Ebony." Then adding, "...we are married." Though not sure why he felt the need to clarify this. "We... Well, we are currently on a quest to catch a cloud. We stopped at the base of the mountain and met with Laissez-Faire, who directed us here. Suggested that you might make clouds of your very own, and that you might have one that we could catch maybe?"

"Ah, Laissez-Faire." Thomas mused, whilst rubbing his chin. "Quite the character I say. Always concerned with buying and selling and buying and selling. Left to her there would be a monetary value to everything, I think. But some things you just can't buy eh."

Charlie took this as a statement rather than as a question.

"So, after a cloud you say. Well, I am sorry to disappoint you, but you have been misinformed by Laissez-Faire. I'm afraid I do not make clouds here. Well, not the sort you are looking for. Sadly, I do not have what you'd hoped for. I do however have steam engines, and it is no doubt the steam from their funnels that has led Laissez-Faire to deduce to you that I make clouds. No, there is only one that can make the clouds, and whilst 'He' is everywhere I'm afraid he is not here right now."

Charlie noticed Ebony flinched, when Father Thomas said he.

"Yes. I'm afraid, for you to acquire the cloud you seek, you will need to progress further up the mountain. Atop sits an ancient castle, very grand it is too. Last I knew it belonged to the Royal House of the Red Dragon, or some nonsense like that. Prince Albert is the chap you need to speak to, I think. Or maybe his mother? Last, I recall she tended to manage things as the Prince is not the best with money. It could have all changed by now though. I don't tend to keep up with current affairs these days. I'm getting on a bit you see. Prefer the company of trains. Old dog and all that eh."

Charlie offered a knowing look and a nod in response.

"Anyway, ha, I digress. Do forgive me. So, the castle sits so high, that from the top of its tallest turret you should have no trouble catching yourself that cloud."

Charlie smiled at this.

"The only issue you are going to have is that the Prince is, unfortunately, quite a greedy fellow. Has an unhealthy attachment to the shiny yellow stuff you see. I trust you have brought sufficient currency to secure your cloud?"

"Well... Um, hmmm... Uh, no. No, we haven't actually brought any money. We kind've assumed you would be able to provide a cloud you see, which is why we brought you this." And here Charlie revealed the tank engine to Thomas.

The Father's eyes lit up immediately and it was clear that he did so desire this tank engine.

"Ha, well." Coughing into his fist. "You are in luck. It just so happens that being a church, we have rather a lot of the shiny yellow stuff stashed here."

"Gold, you mean?"

"Yes, of course. Semantics but yes, I do mean gold. Left over from those pesky Templar days don't you know. I'm not that fond of the stuff myself. I find it rather distasteful. As you already seem to know though I do like train engines. And you happen to have a very fine specimen with you there. I would, in this instance, be quite prepared to offer an exchange. Some of the church's gold for that lovely engine. It will be in the interests of the local community after all."

"Of course." Offered Charlie by way of confirmation.

"However, first I must know whether you are, yourself, God fearing folk?"

"Oh no." Blurted Ebony. Then realised she may have spoken too soon.

"No!" Exclaimed the reverend. "What do you mean no? How can you not believe?"

"Well, I didn't say I didn't believe." Ebony backtracked. "I just said I wasn't God fearing."

Here Charlie smirked to himself.

"Oh, I see. Well, that is good, very good. Of course, God is good of course, and He would not want you to fear him. In fact, I am quite sure that is the last thing he would want but…"

"He?" Questioned Ebony, cutting the father off mid flow.

"Yes, He." Replied Father Thomas. "Everyone knows that God is a man."

"Oh?" Ebony replied. "Is that so? And is that just your God, or all the Gods?"

"I'm not sure I follow you dear."

"Well, first of all I am not your 'dear'. Secondly, what about the Gods Athena, Artemis, Hera and Aphrodite?"

"Ah I see. You are referring, of course, to those Greek goddesses of ancient times. Yes, whilst these are indeed female Gods, we all know now that they were just made-up stories. Mythology that the Greek councils used to strike fear into their citizens and help keep them in check. This is not the same as the real God to which I refer to here."

"Okay. Then what say you of Anubis, Ganesha and Varaha, the animal Gods."

"Ah my dea.. sorry, Ebony. It seems you misunderstand again. These are simply men, turned to animals, using animals for their avatars on Earth. These are not true Gods but merely men, put up on pedestals from which writers of great imagination have taken, and then transformed them, into popular folk tales. There is but only one true God, and He is a 'he'. I mean, he must be. He has a beard for goodness' sake."

"One true God? One true God you say? This being the same God that created the Earth?"

"But of course."

"And the sun?"

"Why yes. The almighty created all things."

"And 'He' then created humans. Is that correct?"

"He started with Adam & Eve, as we all know, yes."

"What about his other suns?"

"Other sons. I'm afraid I don't follow. He only had one son dea..." Thomas managed to catch himself.

"Ahem, Ebony I mean. He only had one son, and that was of course the Lord Jesus."

"No father, you misunderstand me. I meant 'suns'. As in those big shiny balls of fire in the sky. You say God created one especially for us, but what about all of the other suns?"

"I, I'm not sure I follow."

"Suns. You know, those shiny twinkly things you see in the sky at night-time. If 'He' created a sun for us, he then went on to make around 100 thousand million suns for someone else."

"Um, er..."

"And that is just in our little galaxy, the Milky Way."

"Well, I, erm..."

"Let's see." Ebony held up her left hand, fingers spread, tapping the tips of her fingers with her other hand. "There are about two trillion galaxies in the observable universe."

"Um, err, what? Are you sure, that sounds like an awful lot to m..."

"Times that by 100 thousand million and we end up with..." Ebony looked up whilst running the numbers in her head. "We end up with an estimated number somewhere in the region of around 200 billion trillion stars in the known Universe alone."

"I, er, it's just that, um…"

"Every single one of those stars has the potential of its own solar system, and each solar system has the potential for another Earth-like planet, or indeed 'planets', containing life. Just like ours."

"Well, I, when you put it like that, I mean…"

"And you are trying to tell me that with all of those planets out there, with all those suns, with all of that potential for life, all of it unique and all of it wonderful, that you somehow know, based on a tatty old book that you like to read, that God, the God, the one and only true God, is a man, who dresses in a robe and likes to wear a beard!" Ebony, exasperated, threw her hands in the air for emphasis.

"Stop, stop. You are confusing the situation. We are all God's children and, and, and…"

"And, and nothing. We are no more God's children than some bug-eyed alien from the planet Zorg. We are no more God's children than the ant we may carelessly step on and not even notice. We are either all of us God's children or we are none of us God's children.

"But..."

"Don't you think it more likely that God bears no form. Based on the potential infinite number of examples of life, if there is a God, then God is more likely to be an energy of some sort, rather than a bearded old man. The glue that holds the cosmos together. The animating force that makes us aware and drives us forward. The cosmos, in its entirety, experiencing itself through all of us and not just standing over us casting judgements all day long."

"Well, um, you do make a good point I suppose but..."

"If we are all God's children then we are all God together. The idea of a Man and a Woman. Adam and Eve. These are nothing in comparison to the vastness of the infinite everything. Just a teeny tiny minuscule part of the Cosmos." Ebony demonstrates this with thumb and forefinger, held just a smidgen apart, and just a millimetre away from Father Thomas' nose.

"A cosmos." She continued, "that wouldn't even notice should the entire planet Earth disappear with a pop tomorrow. It is clear, Father McKenzie, that you are a good man at heart, but you would do better sticking to your trains if your view of the almighty everything is so limited to a tired old man with a beard."

"I um, I would say I, erm I, ahem, I see."

"To that end father, we have brought for you this train, which we would like to trade you now for some of your gold. We have established already that this is a rare train, one that you desire. Considering our discussions, I have taken the liberty, just now, of christening this train 'Agnos'. 'Agnos the Tank Engine.' You can place him on your tracks and watch him go around and around and around. I would encourage you to listen to Agnos 'tic, tic, tic' along the tracks and contemplate our discussion."

Thus, gold was brought forth by a crestfallen Thomas, the transaction completed, and Agnos set down to 'tic, tic, tic' around Thomas' tracks.

Meanwhile the Earth continued to revolve, and the Universe continued to expand.

Keen to leave on a good note, for Thomas was clearly a good person, who genuinely cared for others, Charlie offered his hand. Thomas took the hand and shook warmly. Charlie thanked him for his time and hospitality and wished him well for the future. Charlie and Ebony then left to continue their quest up the mountain and toward the now fabled Prince.

Politics

'One of the penalties for refusing to participate in politics is that you end up being governed by your inferiors' Plato

Ebony and Charlie continued their ascent. It was not long until they chanced upon their next location. Both were pleasantly surprised to find themselves standing outside of an Inn. By this point they both felt like they could do with a drink, so they decided to go in. They arrived at the door however to find a bit of a commotion occurring.

"If you can't pay for your drinks then you need to sling your hook!"

This was being shouted by a rather burly looking man, escorting a rather less burly looking man out through the door by the scruff of his shoulder.

  "But landlord sir, you know I am good for the money. When have I ever let you down? I just need a little time to collect up some revenue an..."

  "Listen, you've been saying that for weeks now. Not all of us are rich folk you know. Some of us have to actually earn a living. And I ain't doing that if you ain't paying for your drinks now am I? So go on, sling your hook... and don't come back here until you can clear your tab!"

  With that the pub landlord gave the man a final shove through the door and the man, rather ungracefully, tripped and fell, landing in a heap at Ebony and Charlie's feet.

  "I say." Charlie said looking down, "...are you alright down there?"

  "Well." Said the stranger with a smile, "I've certainly been better. Don't suppose you could give me a hand up, could you?"

  The stranger offered up his hand, which Charlie took without hesitation, and then used to help pull the stranger back up onto his feet. Of note, the stranger offered no thanks.

"I'm Charlie." Said Charlie. "And this is Ebony, said whilst gesturing a hand toward Ebony.

"Charmed, I'm sure." Replied the stranger. "Though don't you think you ought to bow as well?"

"Bow?" Questioned Charlie, confused.

"Yes, bow man, bow. That is what your type would normally be expected to do in the presence of royalty is it not." Delivered more as a demand rather than as a question.

"Ohhhh. You must be the prince!' Exclaimed Ebony.

"That's right. I am a prince. A Prince Albert in fact."

"Sounds painful." Muttered Ebony under her breath whilst suppressing a smirk.

"You are not wrong. Carrying the burden of such high status can at times prove painful."

"Ahem. Anyway, Prince Albert, right? We were looking for you and, well, no offence there your lordship, but we don't bow down to anyone. Especially not someone my husband just picked up off the floor."

Red faced the prince retorted. "Is that so? Then I will not spend a second longer in the company of you peasants. Good day."

With that the prince turned on his heel to make off, but before he could Charlie piped up.

"Um, I couldn't help overhearing that you may currently be experiencing some financial difficulties? We might just be able to help you out."

The prince froze. Then turned back around to face Charlie. "Help me out how exactly? Not that I need any help of course."

"Of course, of course. I understand. But should you be in need of some funds, in the short term, like right now I mean. Well, it just so turns out that we have a bag here, full of gold."

At this the prince's eyes lit up.

"We were looking to make an exchange."

"An exchange? An exchange for what?"

"For a cloud."

"For a cloud?"

"Yes, we would like access to your castle."

"You would like access to my castle?"

"Yes. So, we might catch a cloud."

"So, you might catch a cloud?"

"Yes. That's what I said."

"And you need access to my castle because...?"

"Because of the altitude, your mightiness. Because your castle sits at the top of a mountain and from there, we can reach the clouds."

"Oh, I see." Quaffed the prince. "Of course, of course... Makes complete sense now, yes, yes. Okay then, say no more."

At that point the prince placed his arm around Charlie's shoulder.

"Well let's say you start by taking me inside and buying me a drink eh. I can then tell you all about the... ahem, all about my castle then."

The door to the inn was painted black and of a simple wooden design. Two equal sized wooden panels in the bottom half, whilst in the top half was a rose-tinted window, etched with the word 'bar', should anyone be in any doubt as to what was inside. At its centre hung a simple bronze door knocker, shaped as a hoop.

"Appropriate." Mused Ebony, whilst grabbing said hoop and using it to forcefully bash against the door three times.

'Doof, doof, doof.'

The three new friends, for want of a better expression, were soon seated on a small round table, in an area set off slightly behind the bar. Here there was a piano against the wall and an old door that led out into the backyard. Having smoothed things over with the barman, and already used some of the gold to settle the prince's tab, Charlie was able to secure them entry and drinks. These included real ale for Charlie, white pinot grigio for Ebony and a whole bottle of scotch and side jug of water for the greedy prince. Albert also insisted on a pickled egg for a snack. Now settled they could talk and come to an agreement for passage to Albert's castle and to their cloud.

"Okay then." Exclaimed Charlie. "Our thoughts are that you take us to the castle, help us catch a cloud and we give you the rest of the gold. How does that work?"

"Weeellll…" Started the prince started. "There may be a slight issue with that suggestion. I can't deliver specifically what you want. You see, technically it isn't… Well, how can I put this? It's not my… Well, it's just not my castle anymore is all."

"What!" Exclaimed Charlie.

"Now then, here here. No need to panic as I can offer you an alternative."

"But how can you be the prince and not own the castle?"

"Well, it all started a number of years ago you see and... Wait." The prince paused. "How about, I tell you my story, then, in exchange for the rest of that gold, I will give you what you will need to gain passage into the castle? Can't say fairer than that now can I. What do you say?"

Relieved that passage was still a possibility, and with what appeared to be no other choice, Charlie looked at Ebony, who gave a small nod, then reluctantly agreed.

"Oh, come on." said the prince. "Don't look so glum. I'm a member of the elite ruling classes, remember? You can trust me." This was stated with a large Cheshire cat type grin. "Now, the only real question is... Are you sitting comfortably?"

Silence.

"Well, are you?" The prince asked again, this time more forcefully.

"Um, yes, yes." Both Ebony and Charlie agreed.

"Good. Well in that case, I'll begin." And with that the prince began his story.

Dragons & Monkeys I

It began in the olden days, as these things so often do, with stories of poverty, followed by hope and struggle, followed by opportunity, daring and bravery. Ascension by deed, retention by public demand, then by control. Then came deceit, then mistrust, then paranoia. Next came oppression followed by death and war. Always the inevitable and unnecessary war. Eventually things settled into stability and Albert's family, emerging on top, were able to reign, unchallenged, over many centuries.

Inevitably myths and legends grew up around the royal family. One in particular told of how Albert's great ancestor, King Rhuddlan the first, once managed to tame a mighty Red Dragon. Following its capture he used the Dragon as a resource, to keep order in his current territories and gain control of others. He became known as Rhuddlan the Dragon heart, and his estate, thereafter, became known as the 'House of the Red Dragon.'

Here Albert proudly slapped a palm against a crest emblazoning his left breast.

"We were mighty then. Rhuddlan commanded awe and respect. He led with an iron heart. The

House of Red Dragon successfully ruled over these lands for hundreds of years until those monkeys started to meddle, and then a few upstarts got their pants in a twist over taxes and religious bits and bobs. Before you could say boo to a goose the country was being run by an elected parliament and us royals were suddenly taking a back seat. Pah, elected I say. As if that was ever going to work long term."

Ebony and Charlie shared a look.

"Anyway, that was then, and this is now. My father, daddy, the most recent king, passed away recently. By rights, as a man you see, surely, I should have inherited the throne. It was decided however, by that meddling parliament, that mummy should continue to rule as Queen instead. Something about integrity or some other nonsense like that, I don't know."

"Daddy and mummy." Scoffed Ebony. "What are you, five?"

"It's a good point." Chipped in Charlie, ignoring all the previous story. "Why do rich people always refer to their parents as 'mummy and daddy'? I mean, what is that all about?"

Feigning offence, the prince replied. "Well, we can hardly say 'mum' now, can we? That would make us sound like the rest of you pea... I mean, sound like the poor people... You know, like the working class... Like the peasants. How can we be expected to rule if we sound like the people we are ruling over. We can't use expressions like mum, or worse still, 'mam.' People might think we were Northerners! Urgh, goodness no. Or like servants even, heaven forbid. Besides, saying mummy and daddy in public is the quickest way to make you peas... Make the peasants think we are a little tapped. You know, dim witted. Nice, but harmless. Means you don't ever look as closely as you should, because you have already decided we are not that bright. For example, you never question the fact that our faces are all over the money. We let you borrow it, then spend it in our name. Ha, and then charge you taxes for the privilege."

"Wow." Is all Ebony managed.

"Anyway, enough about tedious poor people. I believe I was telling you my story, was I not? How typical of your sort to try and make it all about you."

From here Prince Albert spoke of how his 'mummy' held the throne but did not hold any power. Albert was forced to reside in the background and watch the government of the day collect all of what should have been his family's precious taxes.

Albert then described how he had come up with a plan. First, he was going to unseat the government, then he was going to unseat his mother from power. He would use the good old, tried, and tested tactic of civil unrest.

First of all, he covertly courted what he referred to as, 'fame hungry puppets'. By offering 'royal favours' he manipulated these puppets into persuading the kingdom that it should be independent from its trading neighbours. Despite having enjoyed harmony now for a long time, despite freedom of trade for their economies, and despite freedom of movement for their peoples, the prince, through his puppet master abilities, was able to convince the collective people of the kingdom that they would be better off going it alone.

To help push through his aim he managed to set the stage for his court jester to be elected as the new prime minister for the kingdom. The populous, high on the dizzying visions on an independent utopia, found the jester to be highly amusing. A welcome distraction in fact to the bubbling discomfort that was subconsciously now starting to make itself known. The jester filled his cabinet with an array of clowns from the local Circus. The public did applaud, and a jolly time was being had by all. Independence was thus achieved and the public, most of them at least, applauded the efforts of their great, new, and very entertaining leader.

It was only a matter of time until things fell apart.

Albert explained how he then planned to step in. When the country realised what it had done, he would enter onto stage left and go about bringing order back to the chaos. Through the process he would ascend himself to the throne, demonstrate that parliament was broken and thus, by the will of the people, re-establish the rule of the House of the Red Dragon.

Then the plague happened.

At first there were only rumours of a new and deadly plague, sweeping faraway lands. The Jester and his clown court took no notice of the dark clouds that were gathering. Instead, they threw all caution to the wind, leaving all their ports and trade routes open. They even went so far as to organise a day for their rich friends at the races. By the time the first people started dying it was too late to shut the door. The next two years saw the virus run ravage, taking its toll on the whole kingdom.

Eventually the people no longer felt like laughing. Whilst they had been confined and locked away in their homes the Jester, and his merry band of clowns, had continued to party throughout it all. Finally, he fell out of favour. Instead of looking to Albert though, the clown court got together and, without even consulting the public, elected a new prime minister from their own ranks to lead the land. The new leader came in all guns blazing and within mere weeks had single handedly managed to crash the whole economy.

Another new PM was put into post. The public's opinion again was not considered. The prince could find no traction. Crises after crisis after crisis besieged the land. The rich of course thrived through it all. Inflation boosting their already great accumulations of wealth. The poor, as always, were expected to carry the burdens and pay for the dishonesties that the ruling elite had committed on them. Eventually poverty built to such a level that the poorest in the kingdom no longer felt a part of their own society. They started to down tools and strike and the country eventually ground to a halt.

Still the people would not see Albert as a solution. Not willing to wait any longer Albert now made his play to win favour and seize power. Unfortunately for Albert he had waited too long. The people were done. Instead of being the hero that stepped in to save the day, the prince was now a target along with the rest of the wealthy alumni. Following one particularly dark day for the elite, it was decided by the public that a monkey could do a better job of running the country. It just so happened that a suitable monkey was at hand.

Back in time, alongside the House of the Red Dragon, there had emerged another house. The House of the Blue Monkey. Whereby one sought to rule, the other offered to guide. One wanted to dominate, the other to facilitate. The House of the Blue Monkey was founded upon virtues of trust, courage, love, kindness. Monkey ancestors had only ever sought to heal, to live in harmony with nature and with each other.

"That bloody monkey!" Swore Albert. "He set me up good and proper. Making me take his stupid wager." Rubbing his chin now. "I just don't know how he could have known about the plague."

Anyway, the people, now sick of all the selfishness and greed, did decide to crown the monkey their new king. Albert was evicted from his castle and the Monkey King was handed the keys.

xx lol xx

"So that, you see, is why I don't live in the castle anymore." Finished off the prince.

"Wow." Was all Ebony could manage again.

Charlie, on the other hand, was more curious and wanted to know when all of this had occurred.

"Oh, well, that was some time ago now I would say. Mummy passed just before the eviction. The irony. I would have been king by now if I had just done nothing. Following mummy's death, I never actually had time to get officially sworn in though, so to speak."

"I see." Said Charlie. "And what has become of the kingdom since the Monkey King has been in power?"

"Well, we are reuniting with our neighbours. I hear that trade and commerce have improved again. The standard of living has risen greatly. There is less sickness, almost zero poverty. The climate is improving, and peace has held with little to no political effort."

"So, in sum, the Monkey King is doing a better job?"

"Well, yes maybe. Depends which side of the fence you're on really.

Some of my old hunting buddies aren't that impressed. One of them had to downsize and sell some of his estates recently. Terrible business. Anyway, enough. We made a deal, now hand over the rest of the gold."

"Not so fast." Replied Charlie. "You said you would give me what I needed to gain passage into the castle?"

"Oh yes, I did, didn't I? Okay. I'll tell you what, put the bag of gold on the table and I will put this..." here the prince withdrew a brown hemp bag of his own from his coat pocket, tied and bulging. "I will put this bag on the table at the same time. Here is what you will need to gain passage to the castle."

Charlie was sceptical but agreed and both he and the prince placed their respective bags onto the sticky small round table in front of them. The prince quickly snatched up the bag of gold. Charlie, more gently, picked up the hemp bag. Slowly opening the bag, he discovered it to be full of... "Nuts!" Monkey nuts, to be exact.

"This is just a bag of nuts. What am I supposed to do with these?"

"It is exactly what you will need to gain entrance to the castle."

"But I could have bought a bag of nuts at the bar myself, for a tiny portion of the gold that I have just given to you. How can this be a fair trade?"

"Oh, but my dear boy, who said anything about fair? Also, you are forgetting to factor in the time that I have just afforded you. Do you think people like you ever get to spend time with people like me? Well, you do, but only if you pay for it. And that dear boy is where the rest of the gold comes in. Now, I wish you well in your search for a cloud. If you will excuse me, I feel I've spent enough time in your company and I rather feel like I could do with a wash. Poor has an unpleasant stench to it you know."

Here the prince took his leave, making his way to the other end of the bar where there appeared to be a card game in progress.

"Don't take his nonsense to heart." Said the barperson, now poking his head around the corner. "He's alright really. Got the best interests of the country at heart I reckon."

Ebony's jaw hung down, Charlie finished the rest of his drink, the bar person gave him a wink and a smile.

Standing to leave, Ebony remarked. "Why do you never hear it called a 'Queendom'?"

Virtue

'Monkeys are superior to men in this: when a monkey looks into a mirror, he sees a monkey'
Malcolm de Chazal

Our brave explorers set off from the pub, equipped with their ambition, the clothes on their backs, and a good-sized bag of monkey nuts. As they ascend what is left of the mountain they notice the air cooling, becoming both cleaner and thinner. The background sounds drop away and are replaced with a more peaceful and natural ambience. The views of the surrounding valleys begin to reveal themselves. The climb is exhausting but the combination of all the above is energising.

Soon enough the great castle at the top of the mountain comes into view. The closer they get, the more awe-inspiring it appears. Eventually they find themselves standing at the foot of the castle. On top of the world, they have never felt so small.

After taking a moment to catch their respective breaths, they make their way to the castle entrance. As expected, the castle door was vast. Tall and rectangular in design. Recently renovated and freshly varnished it looked like a very proud door indeed. Cut into the bottom left section of the main door was a little people sized door. This door was already wide open.

"Oh, do you think we can just let ourselves in?" Wondered Ebony aloud.

"Hmm. Can't say I feel comfortable just walking in." Replied Charlie.

"Very well." Said Ebony, now searching for the door knocker.

Ebony spotted the door knock hanging at hand level next to the open door. Ebony was surprised to find the door knock was modest in design (best described as a short pole with a ball at the end) and fashioned out of simple hardwood.

"Nice." Commented Ebony, with genuine respect.

'Doof, doof, doof.'

Ebony stands back, lowers her arms, cups her hands at her front and waits. After several moments a rather small, rather stern looking monkey appeared. Dressed in an orange robe, with space for a tail to protrude from the back, the monkey sported a cleanly shaved head and a serene but focused look in its eyes.

"Can I help you?" Enquired the Monkey.

"Yes." Replied Ebony. "Indeed, you can. We are here to see your master."

"My master?" Questioned the Monkey.

"Yes, your master. Your Boss. 'Thee' boss. The big Man... or the big 'Mon' even. Or the big Man-Key if that is a thing? Is that a thing?" Looking questioningly now at Charlie.

"I'm afraid I do not have a master. Or a boss. Or, as you put it, a man-Key. I am not a pet you see. Neither am I a slave. Nobody owns me, you understand. As for this big 'Man-Key' (this time said using fingers to make quote marks in the air), I will assume you are talking of the king. The Monkey King. Am I right?"

"Ahem. Yeah. Yes, I mean. Sorry. Yes, you are right, of course. My apologies. I didn't mean to offend. It's the clean air, I think. It has made me a little lightheaded."

"That is quite alright, no offence taken. We do especially appreciate the air here. Well then, if you are after an audience with the king, I will assume you have brought with you a suitable offering?"

"An offering?" Questioned Charlie. Then, "...an offering. Yes of course, of course we have an offering. We have brought for your king... Well, for the king that is. We have brought for the king this great bag of... Well, it's a big bag of nuts. Monkey nuts though, of course."

"Of course, of course. Excellent choice." Replied the door monkey. "Well, they will do nicely, very nicely indeed. Well done. Now please hand them over and follow me. Oh, and leave the door open."

With that Ebony and Charlie found themselves on the inside of the castle, following the door monkey. In their minds they had half expected the inside of the castle to be slightly foreboding, cold, grey, and drab. As it turned out the inside of this castle was full of vibrant warmth and colour. Different coloured cottons and silks were draped against the castle walls. Greens, purples, reds, and oranges. Beautifully intricate rugs helped soften underfoot as they walked. Both mature plants and young potted flowers lined the hallways, along with soft furnishings for reclining, padded chairs for socialising and open fireplaces around which souls could gather and share a drink along with a good story or two.

They walked, for what seemed like an age. Whilst on route Ebony felt compelled to ask about the door knock that had impressed her so much.

"We have travelled far and seen many examples. Your abode is surely the grandest of all, yet your door knock has been the humblest. Why is this?"

"The previous occupier used to have a knock fashioned from platinum. Some might say that this is a more valuable material than wood. To these I would simply ask, when in need of heat and shelter, would you rather live on an island rich in platinum or rich in wood?"

"Ahhhh. I see your point." Said Ebony in agreement.

Eventually they reached the heart of the castle. Here, at its centre, was an open courtyard. Brimming with lush greenery, a coy carp filled pond, a network of mini lakes and a gentle waterfall. Bird songs could be heard all about the yard. No wind was there either for the courtyard was completely sheltered upon all sides by the great castle. In the middle of the courtyard stood a beautiful ornate pagoda within which now sat, cross-legged, illuminated, hands palm up, one rested upon each knee, the now fabled Monkey King.

"Hello Sid." Said the door monkey. "I have here some young folks that are seeking an audience with you. Is now a good time?"

"Well, that depends." Replied the king. "What offering have they brought?"

"Well Sid, they have done alright there. They have brought for you a large bag of Monkey nuts."

"Monkey nuts you say? Well in that case show them in, show them in."

Here the door monkey ushered our heroes onto the pagoda and into the presence of the Monkey King. Following this he bowed to the guests and took his leave.

"Greetings." Said Sid. "You are now in session with the Monkey King. What is it I can do for you?"

"Um?" Questioned Charlie. "Did he just call you Sid?"

"Yes, he did." Replied the king.

"Oh, okay then."

"And what is wrong with that might I ask?" Enquired the King.

"Well..." Ebony now chipped in, with a hint of a smile in her voice. "It's not much of a name for a king, is it? Not very 'Kingy' I mean. I think we were expecting something a bit grander. Like Horatio, or something. Or Charles Alexander Tobias the fifth, for example. Sid just sounds a bit, well, a bit normal."

"I see." Said Sid. "Alas, the value we place on a name, or a title does not belie the quality of the person that may reside behind it no? A name is just a name is it not. A title, just a made-up thing we use to identify position and place in a respective hierarchy. It is however what lies at the heart of the soul that will truly define their place in the cosmic order of things."

Charlie rubbed the back of his head. Ebony nodded.

"All of that said, you may be pleased to learn that my full name is Siddhartha Gautama, Monkey King, representative of the House of the Blue Monkey. Though you can call me Sid, for short. Pleased to make your acquaintance."

"Ah, the House of the Blue Monkey thing. We have just been speaking with Albert, from House of the Red Dragon thing. He suggested that you cheated him out of his kingship and castle."

"Cheated? Why would I do that? To cheat is only ever to cheat oneself. I did not cheat Albert of anything but simply invited him to accept a wager that he could not refuse."

"He did mention a wager but didn't really explain what that wager was."

"Well, my new friends, assuming you are sitting comfortably, why don't you let me enlighten you. You see, it began in the olden days, as these things so often do."

Dragons & Monkeys II

Sid regaled them with stories of poverty, followed by hope and struggle, followed by opportunity, daring and bravery. Ascension by deed, retention by public demand, then by control. Then came deceit, then mistrust, then paranoia. Next came oppression followed by death and war. Always the inevitable and unnecessary war. Eventually things settled into stability and Albert's family, emerging on top, were able to reign, unchallenged, over many centuries.

However, through the ascension there was much pain caused. There were many in the land that were simply not interested in the kind of stability that was on offer. The House of the Red Dragon had established a status quo that very much favoured those born of wealth or of those willing to be ruthless in its pursuit. Society, under the Red Dragon, subconsciously came to value traits such as aggression, greed and hostility. For example, what were once simple sports, focal points for community and sharing, were elevated instead to national events, controlled by corrupt organisations. Winners were celebrated beyond reason whilst losers were shamed then forgotten. Honesty and kindness came to be seen more as signs of weakness. Those in society that did not demonstrate the right kind of ambition were now seen as outsiders, fair game to be used in the servitude of those that did.

The mental health of many began to suffer. Aware that they were being taken advantage of, but completely powerless to do anything about it. The confidence for these people inevitably began to wane. Being looked upon as odd, if not obsessed with wealth and status, led many to feel that they just did not fit. Sid's ancestors saw the trend and took it upon themselves to offer spiritual guidance and healing wherever they could.

"We are monkeys but from a different branch. Our eyes turned blue many many moons ago and we, like you, learnt to communicate and share our ideas and develop a society. Unlike you humans we did not turn our back on nature or try to exploit her."

The House of the Blue Monkey continued to exist in harmony with the surroundings, letting societies self-govern and grow organically, based on the collective needs and collective benefits of all. They did not focus on competition or on hero worship. Instead, they focused on equality, happiness, inner peace and love. As they witnessed those in human society beginning to break, they came down from the trees and offered themselves up as an alternative to the way of the Red Dragon. The House of Blue Monkey worked with the disaffected in society and helped them to find and to reach a place. The House of the Red Dragon tolerated the monkeys as they helped to quiet a problem that they had no time for, or indeed no skills to address.

The way of the Blue Monkey simmered, then started to grow in popularity, positioned as it was as a viable alternative to the current status quo. Sensing a growing disquiet in the population the Dragon House decided to take the initiative and offer the populace an alternative to their own rule.

In what can only be described as a master stroke, they sought to buffer themselves against their people by creating a government of the people. They set in motion a series of events that would result in two majority parties, each opposed to the other, each debating and supposedly working in the people's interests. The Dragon encouraged people to stand and be counted as members of these parties, and then invited the remaining public to vote for their favourites. The trick worked, for now the people, instead of hating the House of Dragon for their lot, would turn their angst on whatever party it was that they didn't agree with in this newly named 'House of the Common People'. If they didn't like how the ruling party did things then they would be given a choice, albeit once every four years, to vote for the opposing party. Also, a clever design to ensure no one stayed in power long enough to threaten the Dragon House. Now the King could sit back and manipulate society from afar, whilst the competing parties in the House of the Common People absorbed all the heat. The public now truly believed that they had the power to choose their own rulers.

Successive Royals however started to become lazy. Indeed, they got lazier and lazier, and were more and more happy to leave the tedium of running the nation to those elected government officials. Later, and right under the Dragon's nose, the government, fed up with having to relinquish power every new election, went about creating a new house of their own. Thus the 'House of

Vainglory' was born. Following the end of their respective public careers, the politicians of the day could now shuffle off to the House of Vainglory. It was not necessary to consult the public or to be elected. In addition, whilst serving as politicians, they could ensure entry to the house for all their wealthy chums. Inevitably, in time, this became the true seat of power from which the real decisions were made. Eventually a bill of rights was delivered that gave the House of Vainglory authority over the House of Red Dragon.

"Well." Charlie remarked. "This is all very interesting, but what does all this have to do with today's prince?"

"Well, throughout all this the House of Blue Monkey continued to work in the background. To help and support those that simply did not fit with the created ideals of this governed society. Over time we developed many forms of therapy in our assistance of the people. One of these therapies is known as puppeteering."

Sid described how, by using this therapy, a client can learn to control a puppet that has been fashioned upon themselves. The client will spend time creating stage sets, of differing social situations, and then use their puppet to role play within these sets. This play helps the client to visualise themselves, in those situations, in real life. Eventually, as they learn to manipulate the puppet, to achieve positive outcomes, they in turn learn to develop themselves, in their real-life settings.

"Albert came to me some time ago to enquire about puppet therapy. He had just been passed over by the government as king, in favour of his mother, and he was not feeling very positive about himself. Having to attend many social events the king was concerned that his confidence was starting to suffer, and he could not be seen as weak within his very affluent circles. Our houses have coexisted for many years and Albert felt that he could trust me with his secret. I offered then to take him under my wing and guide him in the art of puppeteering. It transpired that Albert was a natural and he soon made rapid progress."

Sid then explained how there was also a higher level to Puppet Therapy. "If the client is willing to train for many years, they can achieve the status of 'Puppet Master'. A Master is someone who no longer controls only their own puppet, but also can simultaneously control the puppets of others.

A Master can manipulate many puppets at one time and in this way can help positively resolve social conflicts. The prince suggested that he was growing very concerned about how the government at the time was managing the interests of the people. He insisted that he wanted to help. He did not want any credit for this though and wanted to assist in a way that was unseen. He claimed that he wanted the government to function more in the interests of the common people, rather than those interests of vainglory."

"At this point I suggested he should step in, as the future king, and offer to dissolve parliament. He could instead install my house and let the House of the Blue Monkey form a council and implement a different kind of rule. A different way. Albert however insisted that the people were not ready to let themselves be ruled by monkeys and that the idea would never work."

"More fool him." Ebony offered.

"It was at this point that I invited him to take a wager. I would train him in the dark arts of puppet mastery and stand back whilst he manipulated his government. If, however, his manipulations were unsuccessful and if, following this, it should be the will of the people to be led by a monkey, then he would stand aside and relinquish the crown to me. Albert grinned ear to ear, stuck out his hand and we shook on it there and then."

"Confident then?" Observed Ebony.

"Indeed, he was. After he had accepted, we began with his advance training. As I have already said, Albert was a natural at puppeteering. To be a puppet master though you also must study hard. You need to be versed in the disciplines of psychology, sociology, and philosophy. You must understand, when engineering social situations, that every action has a reaction. For every cause there is an effect. For every motion an emotion. For everything a reason. Failing to appreciate this means that an engineered situation can quickly slip out of your control. You soon start reacting to events instead of managing them. Here master becomes slave."

"Sounds risky. How did the prince manage with all that study?"

"Alas, Albert was easily distracted when it came to the study of books. Let's just say that he was never going to be in control of the chaos he ultimately ended up creating."

Sid went on to discuss how it eventually transpired that Albert wanted to tear down the House of Vainglory and that he set about this by throwing the government of the day into chaos. Sid described how Albert had planned to step in at a pivotal point and be seen as the hero of the day. The public would realise this, insist on his ascension to the throne and denounce the government in the same turn. Albert however did not pay attention to events that were manifesting abroad. He failed to understand that spinning the government into chaos would lead to mis-regulation which, whilst normally of little consequence in normal times, would be a very terrible thing when a global plague was starting to take hold. Once the plague had landed on home shores the issue worsened rapidly due to the government being so disorganised. As the plague raged, chaos ensued. Every mess that Albert managed to resolve created adverse conditions that gave rise to two more.

"To cut a long story short, the chaotic rule continued through a number of additional crises and by the time Albert eventually stepped in he had completely lost control of the situation."

"Alas..." chipped in Charley. "The people of the land eventually realised that a Monkey could do a better job."

"That is correct." Confirmed Sid, with a warm and knowing smile upon his face.

xx lol xx

Following this episode Ebony and Charlie properly introduced themselves. They informed Sid about their travels so far and about the purpose of their visit and their wish to finally catch a cloud for Charlie. Once fully up to speed Sid sat for a while in silence with his eyes closed and contemplated. He then reopened his eyes and addressed the pair. Or more specifically addressed Charlie.

"So, young Charlie. I have reflected and I have decided. I can offer you what you need. I will permit you to catch your cloud. There are however some things you must listen to and understand first."

Charlie, beaming now, responded. "Yes. Yes, anything."

"Well, you Charlie, you need to understand that life is essentially played out as four truths. The first, the foundation upon which all else is built, is that existence is suffering. To be here, in these lives, is to be here and to suffer. This is so, as we are all fooled into a constant pursuit, a constant desire, a constant craving for something or for someone. Whether it is lost or unrequited love, or the latest technological gadget, or a big bag of monkey nuts. There is always something we are found wanting."

"Is that why you require people to make an offering, because you are always craving monkey nuts?"

"Ah, no, that is not why. I request offerings as they are good for the karma of those making the offering. That is all."

"Oh." Replied Charlie.

"It does help though that I am partial to the odd monkey nut, but that is beside the point. Anyway, we digress. Back to the principles."

Sid resumed.

"So, then you, Charlie Thatcher, are suffering and you would like to catch a cloud so that you have something to hide the suffering beneath. Whilst I will permit this, here and now, you must work hard to understand the second truth, the truth of the cause of your suffering. Once this is understood the third truth is revealed, the truth to understanding the end of your suffering. You must know that the only way to end your suffering is to let it go. Only when you have blown out the flame will you find what you are truly seeking. For what you are truly seeking you do not yet know. To be enlightened you must indeed follow your own path to its conclusion, the final truth. The cloud you seek will help guide you on this path. This is the reason why the cosmos has brought you here now, to catch your cloud."

Charlie nodded.

"Furthermore, when travelling this path, you should understand that everything that exists is equal, and existence may not be what your mind has led you to believe that it should be. You need to start thinking well of yourself Charlie, and well of all others also. Choose love as your starting point and then build your opinions of others from there. Tell no more lies Charlie. Not to yourself nor to others. Be not unkind and use the gifts of expression to share peace and wisdom. Convey joy to the world and inspire others to do the same."

Charlie nodded, to show he understood.

"Understand that everything that happens to you will be as a consequence of your own behaviour. You always have a choice, Charlie. In those rare moments when choice is taken from you, it will have been the choices you made before that would have led you there. When you offer your services to another in trade, do so with honesty and integrity and with the genuine intention and hope that what you do will in some way benefit others whilst benefiting yourself. Never fail to try hard. Understand that a failure is a success when every effort has been made. We can only fail when we do not try. When every effort continues to be made, all failures can be overcome. Be always calm and take time, where you can, to rest your mind. Embrace your senses and let yourself become aware of the sounds, the sights and the smells that constantly surround you. Finally, Charlie, learn to let all that noise from within fade away. Spend time to focus on your thoughts and feelings. Organise these, as you would organise anything in the outside world. Slowly, but surely, each can be stored in a rightful place and your inner self can become calm. Understand these principles my friend and your journey will indeed prove fruitful."

"Wow." Said Charlie. "Those are wise words, I agree. But what if I am unable to heed and master these truths. What then?"

"Well then, Charlie, I will see you back here in your next life, and we shall have this conversation again."

Following their talk Sid led Charlie and Ebony up onto the rooftop of the castle. The highest point of the castle sat above the clouds. They were in fact now looking down onto a sea full of clouds, as one might look down onto a pond full of fish. Charlie was handed a net, like a butterfly net, that sat at the end of a pole. A very very long pole.

"Well, this is your moment, Charlie. This is what you came here for. Go catch yourself that cloud and make sure you catch the right one for you. You will only get one attempt at this."

"Alrighty then." Said Charlie excitedly. "Ebony, what do you think? Which cloud should I go for? There are so many."

At this very moment a single cloud caught Ebony's eye. It appeared smaller than the rest, and for a second seemed to be drifting alone, in its own patch of blue sky.

"There is Charlie." Pointed Ebony. "Over there. That's the cloud. That little white fluffy one. That's the cloud you should catch."

"I see it." Confirmed Charlie. And without further ado he cast his net. His aim was true, his hand steady. The net swung the first time over and neatly embraced the small cloud within its grasp.

"YES!" Exclaimed Charlie. "Whoop whoop! First time Ebony, first time. Did you see that, I mean did you see th..."

Charlie turned, but Ebony was no longer there.

"What the..." Turning now to the Monkey King. But he too had faded and was no longer there.

'What is going on,' thought Charlie to himself, just before he noticed the ground beneath his feet beginning to fade and disappear.

Panic started to rise in Charlie's throat, and he gripped hard onto the net handle, still within his hands. He clenched his eyes and closed them tight, as tight as he could.

The world around him faded to nothing and then Charlie woke up.

Awakening

*'This terrifying world is not devoid
of charms, of the mornings that
make waking up worthwhile'*
Wislawa Szymborska

A cough.

"Ahem, excuse me."

No answer.

A slightly louder cough.

"Ahem. Sir, excuse me but..."

No response.

A very loud cough.

"AHEM! Sir. WAKE UP!"

With this Charlie came too with a jolt.

"What the, um, er, um, who the... Ebony. Where is Ebony? The Monkey king, where... What is going on? Why does everything ache? I must have dozed off."

Charlie then looked in the direction of the voice that had just woken him.

"What the...!" Exclaimed whilst backing away.

"It's you. You are the clou... You, you... You are here. But how? How are you here? And how are... How are you... How are you doing that?"

"Doing what?" Came the reply.

"How are you talking to me? You are talking to me, aren't you? At least I can hear you talking to me."

"Of course, I'm talking to you. How else are we going to communicate?"

"But, but... You're a cloud!" Exclaimed Charlie.

"So I am." The cloud replied.

"But you don't even have any lips." Replied Charlie.

"Of course I don't." Replied the cloud. "I'm a cloud. Why would I want lips? If it helps, I can make some lips. We clouds are very good at making shapes, don't you know."

"No, no. There's no need, no need for that. But how can I hear you? Are you in my head?"

"Kind of. Have you ever heard of telepathy?"

"Yes, yes. Of course, I have heard of telepathy. I'm not stupid."

"Okay, good. Good for you. Well, I am using telepathy to talk to you now." Telepathed the cloud.

"Right." Said Charlie. "Only, I don't know how to talk telepathy. I'm a human you see."

"So you are. Well done!" Exclaimed the cloud. Then, "...actually, humans do know 'how to talk telepathy.' It was in fact how your ancestors used to communicate, before you got all territorial, power and wealth oriented. As a race you used to collectively share your thoughts and ideas, which is what helped you evolve. Then, at some point, you started inventing 'talk out loud' languages, so you could all have secret conversations instead."

"What!" Scoffed Charlie. "That's ludicrous."

"What, more ludicrous than a talking cloud?"

"Ah." Said Charlie. "I suppose you have a point."

"Anyway." Replied the cloud. "You can call me Jacob. And it is me that should be questioning you by the way."

"Oh, that is a nice name for a cloud. And you can call me Charlie. Charlie Thatcher. You know, I had no idea that clouds could have names. Especially human ones. I suppose you would have names, but I would have expected odd cloudy ones. Certainly not a name like Jacob."

"Yes." Replied Jacob. "Indeed. But back to my questions. For starters, what on Earth am I doing here, floating about inside your living room?"

"Ah, well..." said Charlie, shifting uncomfortably. His worn armchair let out a creak. "About that. You see. Well, you see, you are here because... Well, because I caught you. Just now. Or just then even. Back at the Castle. The Monkey Castle. In a net. In a fishing net. In a cloud fishing net. It was a very good net. Attached to a very long pole and... Well, I went to the Castle with Ebony, looking for a cloud to catch, and I caught you. Somehow, I appear to have brought you home with me."

"You must have caught me napping." Said Jacob. "I must have drifted off. No pun intended."

"Drifted off?" Questioned Charlie. "I didn't know that clouds could sleep."

"Well, what do you know? You didn't know clouds could talk and have names either, but you do now."

"Ahem. Yes." Conceded Charlie.

"Well Charlie? What is it that made you think it would be okay to catch me in the first place? And more importantly, why?"

"Well." Started Charlie. "It's like this. Um, in fact it's a little embarrassing now. Now I know you can talk and have a name n' all. You see, I didn't know clouds could talk when I..."

"Yes Charlie. We have already established that fact. But why am I here?"

"Of course, of course. Well Jacob, um, you see... I don't know if you know, but I don't like to go outside you see."

"I don't understand. If you don't like going outside, how did you catch me?"

"Well, I do go outside. Of course, I do. But I don't like to. Well, not in the daytime at any rate. It's fine to go out in my dreams but in real life it's, um... Well..."

"Right." Replied Jacob.

"So, you see, I thought... Well, that is, I decided... If I could catch myself a cloud then I could, you know, go out in the daytime, and take my cloud with me. To block out the sun and stop other people from looking at me you see? So nobody would look at me. It was Ebony's idea. She always said I lived under a cloud anyway. So, I thought, you know, well, why not?"

"So, nobody would look at you?"

"Yes, so nobody would look at me, that's right. I planned to tie a silver string to you. Then use you, a bit like an umbrella, you see? To block out the sun. So nobody would look at me anymore."

"Of course!" Exclaimed Jacob. "I totally get it now. I mean, why would anyone want to look at a man walking down the street with a cloud floating above his head? There is of course nothing remotely curious about such a sight."

"Well, when you put it like that, I suppose…"

"I mean, really? If you don't want to draw attention to yourself then not walking down the street with a cloud tied above your head is a pretty good place to start."

"Okay, okay." Said in agreement, though a little emotional now.

"And tying me with a piece of string? What is that all about? I'm a cloud, not a balloon."

"Oh, do you have balloons where you come from then?"

"Where I come from! You mean 'here'. Here is where 'we' come from Charlie. I come from the same place as you. And yes, we have balloons. An annoying amount of them in fact. You humans like to regularly release them into the sky for some reason."

"Ah, yes, sorry about that. But anyway, my point was that I just can't stand being out there anymore. You know, with people staring at me and with the sunlight heating my face and glaring in my eyes. I hate it you see, and I just don't want to be seen. At least with a cloud hanging over me I wouldn't feel the sun and, and, even if they did see me, I wouldn't see them."

Seeing Charlie upset, Jacob softened his tone a little and instead asked Charlie to explain why he didn't like to feel the sun and why it was that he wanted to hide, or rather not be seen by others. It transpired that since Ebony had passed Charlie had started to go out less and less. Ebony was his world, and without her his world had ceased to exist and slowly, day by day, Charlie had ceased to exist with it. The world, in turn, had started to forget about Charlie.

Out of necessity the furthest Charlie would ever venture now was to the end of his street. Even this journey was becoming too much for him. He hated the way that heads would turn in his direction as he shuffled through the shadows. He knew that they stared at him. He knew that they were judging him. He felt their cold minds and occasional pity. He knew that they judged him a failure.

In the queues at the post office, he sensed those about him turning their noses in disdain at the odours he was no doubt omitting. At the fish and chip shop, he would stand alone in the queue whilst others engaged in conversations as to the weather, the price of fuel and various sports, for which, in fairness, he had never held any real interest. The young girl that served Charlie in the chip shop was in fact the only soul he'd had any kind of relationship within recent years. She seemed to be the last kind soul alive and would always share with Charlie a warm smile. He had no idea why.

So it was, proclaimed Charlie, that he had set his sights upon catching himself a cloud. He was done with the world and the world, it seemed, was done with him. While he must be here, continue to be here, continue to breathe, to exist and to be, then he would do so without the light and live out his days, as he rightfully should, underneath his very own cloud. No one again would ever have to set eyes upon his face. If nothing else, it would spare the poor girl at the chip shop the burden of having to smile at him once a week.

When Charlie had finished with his explanation Jacob let out a long sigh.

"That, Charlie Thatcher, might be the saddest thing I have ever heard."

"Really?" Replied Charlie.

"No." said Jacob. "No, of course it isn't. Not by a long shot."

"Oh."

"You see, I've been a cloud for a long time now Charlie, and I can tell you that I have heard it all before. All this nonsense, I have heard all of it before."

"Ah, right." Said Charlie, rather off put. "But whether you've heard it all before or not, what am I to do? I still wanted my cloud, and I can barely keep you now. Not a talking cloud, with a name. I mean, that just wouldn't be right."

"So, what you're saying Charlie, is that you still want to have a cloud, just not a talking one?"

"Right." Said Charlie.

Curiously, at this point, Charlie began feeling, for the first time in a very long time, the slightest twinge of excitement in his chest.

"Okay. Fair. Well then, the only true way to be in possession of a cloud is to first fully understand and appreciate what a cloud is. Don't you agree?"

"Right." Agreed Charlie, this time with some enthusiasm. Again, he felt, if he wasn't mistaken, just a little bit more excited than before. "So, how do we do that then?" He asked eagerly.

"Well Charlie in my experience, which we have already established is great, is that if you want to understand a cloud, you first have to be a cloud."

"Oh." A pause followed. "Did you just say, 'be a cloud'?"

"Yes Charlie. To keep a cloud, you first need to be a cloud."

"Right." Said Charlie for a third time. At the same time, he felt the minute spark of excitement extinguish and deflated slightly into a slump.

"Charlie, what is the matter? Do you not want to be a cloud? I mean, just for a little while. So, you can see just what it is that us clouds do."

"Well, it's not that I don't want to be a cloud specifically,'' said Charlie. "It's just that you seem, you know, like you are... You know, obviously... Well... Completely mad. I am a human you see, so how on earth can I be a cloud?"

"Oh, is that all? Charlie, you just have to trust and come outside with me."

"Outside? Outside, yes, that's another thing. It has obviously slipped from your fluffy mind already, but in case you weren't listening the first time. I DON'T LIKE GOING OUT!"

"Ah." Replied Jacob unperturbed. "What you actually said was that you didn't like going out in the daylight. Am I right?"

"Yes." Said Charlie. "And it is daylight now."

At this point Charlie stood, shuffled to the window, and yanked open a curtain. He was surprised to see that a thick fog had settled outside.

"But, but I don't understand. It was bright daylight when I looked out earlier."

"Maybe it was Charlie. But what does it matter? There is a thick fog now. A fog so thick that I can assure you not one soul will witness your presence if you come outside with me."

Charlie suddenly felt like he had no choice but to relent. Drawing a deep breath, he thus began to prepare himself for a new venture into the outside world.

Rising

'Our greatest glory is not in never falling, but in rising every time we fall' Confucius

Charlie, having shuffled into the hallway, took his best outside coat from the hanging hook. His best coat was of course his only coat. Stained and torn, smelling of musk and mould. Loose change in one pocket, stale crusted tissue in another. Not fit for a pet to sleep upon, it made Charlie feel safe and secure. Security was what Charlie needed to feel right now, if he was going to go outside with the cloud, so he took a deep breath and put it on. Next, he reached for his trusted cane.

"You won't be needing that where we are going." Jacob told him.

Leaving the cane where it was then, Charlie flicked the catch on the door and unhooked the rigid security chain. With a protesting creak the door opened, and Charlie stepped out into the world.

In front of Charlie lay a short, cracked weed encrusted path, leading to a set of three fat concrete steps, which in turn lead to the main outside street pavement. Complementing the steps was a rusted steel handrail which Charlie now gripped onto tightly, sweaty hands soaking up some of the rust into deeply aged grooves. Fortunately for Charlie he knew these steps well for, as it was at that moment, he could barely sense them under foot. Reaching the last step there was no need to open the gate, for the gate was not closed. The weeds and the rust held it open, like some obliging doorman maybe hoping for a tip, or better still, to be dismissed and put out of their collective misery. Charlie gingerly shuffled onto the pavement and was relieved to find Jacob there when he eventually looked up.

"So?" Questioned Charlie.

"So what?" Questioned Jacob.

"Well, I'm here. You got me outside. Now what?"

"Now we wait."

"Wait for wha..."

Before the question had fully left his lips Charlie became aware of a shadow. Aware of a presence approaching through the thick dense fog.

"Who is that?" Charlie asked nervously.

The figure drew closer, the fog became denser.

"Who is that?" Charlie asked again, more demanding this time and now with a hint of fear encroaching on his voice.

"Have no fear." Replied Jacob. "Have no fear."

The figure, no more than three metres away now, began to reveal itself. Tall and thin, slight but massive. The figure donned a mask, the type a quack doctor would have worn in the plagues of old. Something that one might witness in a night terror, only here it was somehow not so scary. Hair flowed, long and grey about the mask, soft but unkempt, resting upon broad shoulders. A style of top hat was worn on top of the head. For attire, what might have been a robe in days long past was now a long dark brown leather dress coat, reaching just below the knee line. The coat was buttoned but open, to reveal a smart Victorian style waistcoat, made from fine deep blue wool, on top of a stiff collared white floral-patterned shirt, highlighted by a gloriously flared silken silver cravat. The trousers fitted well against strong legs, pinstriped in style and cut loose at their bottoms. As a final point of note the figure appeared to be sporting a pair of quality leather boots, supported by the clean heavy click, clunk of wooden heel meeting concrete, the accompanying gait oozing confidence.

The figure continued to approach Charlie and the fog was so thick now that the figure was all Charlie could make out. Panic gripped but Charlie was too old and weak to turn and run so he stood, frozen to the spot, and prepared to meet what he now thought might be his maker. At that moment the figure stopped and slowly raised its arms. Charlie thought of zombies, or Frankenstein maybe, who was a zombie of sorts. It was then that Charlie saw.

"Oh my God!" He said out loud. "What is... I mean... What are... They can't be..."

"Oh, but they can." Jacob confirmed.

"But it... It looks like... I mean... It looks like..."

"That's right Charlie. Behold Lord Gangles. Lord Gangles who have wind chimes for fingers."

Utterly flabbergasted and transfixed now on those beautiful fingers, Charlie sensed the wind suddenly pick up around him and somewhere, in the distance, the soft sound of chiming music began to play. Charlie fell into a reverie, a trance of sorts. As the wind grew stronger the music grew louder. The fog was so dense now that Charlie could not see a thing. Not Lord Gangles, not the world, not the ground beneath his feet. Not even Jacob who had led him here. Instead, he stood stock still and became aware of an ever-growing sense of peace and tranquillity growing inside of him. He was at peace and slowly a sensation of floating began to make itself known.

Soon after Charlie realised that the fog was starting to thin. At this he snapped out of his reverie and attempted to regain his bearings. He looked ahead, but still could not see clearly. He looked side to side, but still, he could not see clearly. He looked up, but above was only sky. He looked down, but he could not see clearly. Or could he? Actually yes, yes, he could. Charlie could now clearly see the pavement. This was as he expected. However, his feet were no longer on that pavement and that pavement was getting further and further away with every passing moment.

He looked ahead, and now he could see clearly. Not the houses across the street but the sky. He looked side to side, and now he could see clearly. Not the parked cars that lined the road, of the old trees that ran through the pavements, but the sky. He looked up and above was still only sky. He looked back down, and now he could see clearly. He really could see. He could see everything. Not just his street but the whole town. He could see the park, he could see the shops, he could see all the streets of houses. The greys and the greens and the blues that ran through it all.

He felt light, light as a feather. He felt no pain, all aches and complaints had gone. He felt young, like all the energy of the cosmos was there at his disposal. He felt free, the fear could not touch him at this moment now. He sensed his body, his shape, his being, but had somehow lost his form. He went to speak, to shout out in delight. At this moment he realised he no longer had a mouth.

"Use your mind." Came a cry.

'Of course,' thought Charlie, 'telepathy.'

"That's right." Replied Jacob. "You've got it."

'Got what?' Thought Charlie. 'Did he just hear that?'

"Of course, he did." Replied Jacob with a smile. "I'm telepathic, remember?"

"Ha ha!" Charlie exclaimed, now with a broad smile painted on his own non lips. "This is amazing. I don't know what you did, or how you did it, but this is amazing! This feels... Amazing! Am I actually a cloud now?"

"Yes." Confirmed Jacob. "To all intents and purposes Charlie, you are. At least for now."

"But I want to stay a cloud forever! I don't remember ever feeling this alive."

And there lies the problem, thought Jacob, only this time to himself.

"So?" Charlie questioned. "What now?"

And with that, Charlie's time as a cloud began.

Seeing

'I dreamed I was a butterfly, flitting around in the sky; then I awoke. Now I wonder: Am I a man who dreamt of being a butterfly, or am I a butterfly dreaming that I am a man?
Zhuangzi

After some basic orientation exercises in the practice of cloud movement (float up, float down, float left, float right) Charlie was ready to be introduced to some of the other clouds in the sky. Jacob led Charlie toward a large incoming pack of white fluffy clouds. Charlie was awestruck. Of course, he had observed clouds from the ground before. He had even observed clouds from an aeroplane before. But he had never witnessed, or even thought to see, just what a large pack of clouds might look like to another cloud. Especially to a new cloud, seeing clouds for the first time.

As they ventured closer Charlie noticed differences amongst the pack. There were big clouds, small clouds, fat clouds and thin clouds. Chunky, wispy, lumpy and misty. All handsome, pretty, bountiful, and beautiful. For years Charlie had walked the Earth below, as clouds passed up above. Whilst he had looked up, every now and then, he now realised that he had failed to ever take the time to look up and see. To look properly and truly see the glory that he was witnessing now.

Jacob took Charlie straight to the front of the pack. As a new cloud it was custom for him to first meet and be introduced to the pack guide.

"She goes by the name of Walker." Jacob told him.

"Walker?" Smirked Charlie. "That's a funny name for a cloud."

"Why do you say that?"

"Well, she doesn't have any legs for a start. Oh, and well, because you clouds don't walk do you. Because your clou..."

"Okay Charlie, point made. But she was hardly going to call herself 'floater' now was she?"

"Ah, yes I see." Charlie conceded. "But still, why Walker? Of all names, that still seems very strange for a cloud."

"Stranger than Jacob?"

"Ahem. Hmm."

"Tell you what, why don't you ask her yourself?"

Here Jacob introduced Charlie to Walker.

Pushed to describe Walker, Charlie would have said tall, maybe a little geeky and uncomfortable looking. She wore an aura of kindness but did not display the cocky outward confidence that Charlie was used to seeing in the leaders on land. When Charlie introduced himself, he noticed that Walker was avoiding eye contact.

"You're not a cloud, you're a human pretending to be a cloud."

"Well, yes." Charlie confirmed, caught a little off guard.

"You are pretending to be a cloud because you want to know what it is like to be a cloud."

"Well, yes, I um..."

"You want to know what it is like to be a cloud so you can decide whether or not it is morally correct to keep a cloud of your own." This was not a question.

"Well, I um…"

"Effectively you would like to enslave a cloud."

"Now look here." Charlie started. "I do not wish to enslave anyone. I simply wanted too… Well, I wanted to… You know, I… Um… Why are you called Walker?"

Not the most subtle change of conversation but effective, nonetheless.

"My name is Walker after the famous Jedi Knight, who was called Luke Skywalker and who saved the Jedi from the evil Empire and from Darth Vader who turned out to be Luke Sky Walker's father. But Darth Vader is not my father because I am a cloud."

"Oookay… That is interesting. I didn't know that clouds were watching movies.

"Luke Skywalker was trained by Yoda. We do not know where Yoda comes from. Yoda is a Jedi Master. Yoda is green."

"Yes. Green. Indeed."

"Yoda lived to almost 900 years old. That is very old to a human but not very old to a cloud. Yoda was not a cloud."

"Well, yes. You don't see many green clouds now do you?"

"There are no green clouds in the daytime but sometimes in the night-time there are green clouds in Iceland."

"Ah yes, the Northern Lights."

"Yes, the aurora borealis. They are clouds and they are green, and they appear only at the poles. It is very cold at the poles."

"Cold, yes. It is a little chilly in those places for sure. Do you feel the cold then?"

"The South pole is colder than the North pole. It is too cold for humans there but not for clouds."

"Too cold for humans you say."

"Yes. It is too cold for humans unless they have very warm clothes on them to keep them warm."

"Ah..."

"You are a human so you would need very warm clothes to go there. Although today you are a cloud so I suppose you could..."

Charlie was getting a little tired of this conversation but wanted to know more about how Walker had come to learn of Star Wars.

"So, Walker." Charlie interrupted. "How on Earth did you learn about Luke Skywalker and Yoda?"

"I watched them at the cinema. The cinema is a big screen that plays movies and has loud noises, which I normally do not like but at the cinema they make sense and sound good."

"Yes, well, I know what a cinema is... I just don't remember the last time I saw a cloud in the audience. Next you will be telling me you ate popcorn there too."

"I would not eat Popcorn. Popcorn cloud is my friend. Sometimes Popcorn comes to the cinema with me to watch Star Wars."

"No, that's not what I... Ah, but... hmm... No, just forget it."

"In the cinema there are lots of cars too. Popcorn likes to look at the different cars. They are not like the old cars that were pulled by horses."

Of course, Walker was talking about a drive-in cinema.

"You think that clouds cannot do the same things that humans do."

"Well, you do live in the sky."

"Clouds live in the sky. Living in the sky means clouds can see everything that humans do."

"Yes, okay but..."

"Luke Skywalker is cool. I am cool. I am in the sky. Therefore, I am Walker."

"Right. Fair enough. Can you do any Jedi mind tricks?"

"No. I am a cloud."

At this point Charlie made good his excuses and asked Jacob if they could maybe move on and meet some of the other clouds. After floating far enough away Charlie said to Jacob.

"Well, she's a little odd."

"Odd. That is indeed one word Charlie, yes."

"Well, I mean, she's a little odd to be a leader don't you think?"

"Leader Charlie? Who said Walker was a leader?"

"Well, I, I just assumed. You took me to see her first so I assumed she must be your leader, no?"

"No Charlie. We are clouds. We do not have leaders. We have been around way long enough to know that leaders don't work. Where there is a leader there will always be another, wanting to lead, willing to destabilise all and everything to become the next leader."

"Oh."

"Where there is a leader there will always be hardships and pain, save those privileged few that work to maintain their chosen leader's will. No Charlie, we have long since abandoned leaders and are weary of any that would wish to be one."

"So, what is Walker then?"

"Walker is instead our moral compass. Our guide, to whom we look to for inspiration. As to whether Walker is odd, well that my friend is simply a matter of opinion. You see, humans have short life spans, therefore they have short memories. Humans are reliant on words and pictures for their history. Words and pictures chosen by those who go before them. Their realities can sometimes be skewed, depending on how those before them chose to present those words and pictures."

"I'm not sure I follow." Said Charlie.

"Well, to cut to the chase. What you might see as odd, we might see as special. What you might determine is a regression, we might determine is an evolution. You may say that something is broken, we may be more inclined to say that something has been fixed."

"Still not sure I follow. And that doesn't change the point that Walker is a little odd to be a leader, or a guide or whatever."

"Walker, Charlie, is the most fair and honest cloud I have ever met. Walker is the most ingenious cloud I have ever met. Walker knows neither ambition nor violence. I would say her imagination is boundless, coupled with the willingness and single-minded determination to make any imagining a reality. Put quite simply, she is the best moral guide that there could possibly be."

"Oh." Responded Charlie.

"Imagine, for one moment, that humans had guides that they knew would not lie to them. People they could follow that were not driven by their own empty self-interests. People to follow that they knew would only ever have their best interests at heart. Just imagine the progress your species could make if all the 'leaders' of your so-called civilised world were like Walker."

"Well, when you put it like that, I can certainly see the appeal. Alright then. Viva Cloud Walker!"

"Still not sure you're getting my point there Charlie, but yes, why not. Viva cloud Walker. Viva Cloud Walker indeed."

High Society

Jacob then led Charlie on through the pack, stopping and chatting with clouds as they went. One of the first clouds they spoke to was a delightful lady cloud named Lily. Young in spirit, light and free. She was of course white, like the others, but seemed to glow a little on the inside. She radiated warmth and kindness, her telepathic smile infectious.

"So, Charlie, how long have you been a cloud then?" Lily asked.

"Well, this is actually my first day."

"Oh my." Said Lily. "You seem to have mastered the basics very quickly. You are obviously a natural. And tell me, how are you enjoying being a cloud so far?"

"Well, it's a little early to tell just yet. I mean, I already love being a cloud but I'm not totally sure about the company yet."

"Oh." Replied Lily, a little offended.

"No no," said Charlie. "Present company accepted. I mean, you seem wonderful. Well, I mean, I like you. Well, of course I like you but not in that way of course. I'm married, don't you know."

With a soft smile Lily offered some reassurance.

"It's okay. I understand. I believe you have met Walker already?"

"Yes, yes, I have. She seems a nice enough cloud but I'm not altogether sure if she is leader material. Or guide material. Or whatever. Anyway, she has a rather unhealthy fascination with Star Wars."

At this Lily let out a soft giggle.

"You will find most clouds have an obsession with the stars Charlie."

"Really?"

"Well, there is a certain amount of jealousy amongst us clouds towards the stars. I mean, when was the last time anyone told you to reach for the clouds. You'd think they would tell you that, seeing as though we are a lot closer. But no. It's always about the stars, Charlie. Star this, star that. Always positive and always exciting. You see, we live in the sky too Charlie, but people don't seem to notice us in the same way. In fact, human folk often get positively grumpy when we come out. Yet when the stars are out, they get all gushy."

It was clear to Charlie that he had hit upon a rather sore spot, and he began to wish he had never mentioned Star Wars. He did however want to know more.

"So, what exactly is it you dislike so much about the stars? I mean, you can't deny that they are beautiful."

"That's just it Charlie, they are beautiful. They say each star is the soul of a person that has either lived on this planet or on another. Freed from life's shackles they can explore the entire universe, at their own leisure, forever and ever until the end of time. Or until they choose to live again. In another life."

"But that's amazing!" Exclaimed Charlie. "Why would you not like that?"

"Because we are not 'persons' Charlie. We are clouds. And we clouds... Well, we clouds are stuck here, on Earth Charlie. We only get to fly so high and then we must stop. This planet is beautiful, and we are lucky and blessed to be here. Most of us though can't help feeling a slight pang of jealousy, Charlie. Jealousy that we can never explore the wonders of the Universe like your race can. Like human souls do. Do you understand?"

Suddenly it became clear. Charlie was enjoying being a cloud so much already, he had forgotten how blessed he had been to be a human. To live for only a finite number of years. Nothing but a brief spark in the darkness. A beautiful light in a beautiful moment, then free. Free to leave and explore the Universe forever. Well, if what Lily said was true of course.

It seemed now however that the clouds were instead tied here to the Earth. Tied to the planet and whatever fate may become of it in the future. How many human lifetimes would that be? Well, humans dying to become stars certainly was a nice idea, and Charlie was grateful for it. But if there were any truth in this then why hadn't he known about it already? Why didn't the humans talk about it? No, Charlie was much smarter than that so at this point he opted to bid Lily a farewell and continued his journey through the pack.

Next Charlie came upon a group of clouds. Much smaller and lighter, sprightlier, and quicker than the others. It dawned on Charlie that these must be children. Child clouds, who knew? Charlie decided to settle where he was and watch them play a while.

"Look. What am I?" Demanded Toby Cloud.

"Um…" "Er…" "Hmmm…" Were the replies.

"Oh, oh, I know. Me, me, me…" shouted Smudge Cloud excitedly.

"You're a cat!"

"Yes!" Exclaimed Toby. "Meow." Added for extra effect.

"I thought you were an Ephelump." Said Jazz Cloud.

"An Elephant you mean?" Corrected Toby Cloud, rather teacher like.

"Well, you were too fat to be a cat." Jazz Cloud said confidently.

"I was a fat cat." Toby Cloud retorted. Adding, "…cats can be fat you know?"

"Like a fat tiger!" Chipped in Indie Cloud excitedly.

"Yes Indie. Like a fat tiger, exactly. Not an Ephelump. Elephant, I mean. That's just stupid."

"You're stupid." Said Jazz Cloud.

"No, you are." Replied Toby Cloud.

"No you are." Said Jazz Cloud back.

"Well, if you're so clever, let's see what you can do." Challenged Toby Cloud.

"Pah. Okay. Watch this."

And with that Jazz Cloud began to change shape. She stretched herself out into a long thin shape.

"A snake!" Shouted Toby Cloud.

"Wrong." Replied Jazz Cloud, as she continued to change shape. Now adding what appeared to be a body to a long neck.

"Oh, oh, oh... A beautiful white swan" Offered Indie Cloud, again rather excitedly and appearing to do a little dance at the same time.

"Wrong again." Said Jazz Cloud. Now she added a small head to what was obviously a neck, and four long legs to the bottom of what was obviously now a body.

"A dinosaur?" Suggested Smudge Cloud.

"Wrong."

"A lifting crane then?" Offered Smudge Cloud this time.

"A lifting what?" Toby Cloud questioned, in a rather sarcastic tone of cloud voice. "You do know that a lifting crane isn't an animal, don't you?"

"So?"

"Well, we are playing guess the animal shape. Not, guess the big metal mad man-made shape."

"Well, she looks like a lifting crane!" Said Smudge Cloud defiantly.

"Wow. And I thought Jazz cloud was stupid."

"I'll tell you what's stupid. This game is stupid. That's what's stupid, and I don't want to play anymore."

"Good. You're rubbish at it any...."

"A GIRAFFE!" Yelled Indie Cloud, again accompanied by a little jig. "Jazz is a Giraffe and I'm the winner."

"No you're not." Said Toby Cloud. "I was about to say that. Until 'El Stupido' said she was a crane."

"Well, I said it first." Confirmed Indie Cloud aloud. "Didn't I Jazz? didn't I? I said you were a giraffe first so that means I'm the winner."

And so it went. On... And on... And on...

Charlie, reflecting now on past decisions made, felt both blessed and undeserving, to be able to float and observe the cloud children play. Today, here and now, Charlie felt he had all the space and time in the world. As he sat and watched he felt his heart fill with joy at the innocence of it all, offering a little silent prayer that these cloud children might always retain an element of their endearing innocence. A light that they may follow where roads ahead may darken.

Contemplation concluded, Charlie let go a sigh and felt now was the right time to move on. With Jacob now somewhere ahead of him he followed and made his way back through the pack, meeting a whole variety of different clouds on route.

First there was Hazy, an aged male hippy cloud. In fact, hazy wasn't sure if he was a real cloud at all, suggesting he might instead be just a cloud of smoke.

"Like hey Charlie dude, you're a cloud. Like that is totally far out. Others tell me I'm a cloud but I think I'm more like a ball of beautiful sweet smelling smoke, just experiencing myself as a cloud you know. Like as part of a cosmic stream of consciousness that only exists so it can witness itself. You know, like God dude, like totally God. We are all just wisps of smoke blowing on the cosmic breeze man. Let it in Charlie dude. Let it in and let go. Groovy!"

Next came Fizzy. A younger lady cloud, resembling a very bad hair day and with a personality to match.

"Hi Charlie. Pleased to meet you. My name is Fizzy, rhymes with dizzy, though I don't know why they call me that. Not that they do call me that of course, it's just that dizzy does rhyme with fizzy, so why wouldn't they call me that, you know. Dizzy Fizzy, or busy Fizzy. Busy fizzy sounds better, right? Busy rhymes too you know, though you would need to spell busy with a 'Zee', otherwise it just wouldn't look right, because fizzy is spelt with two Zees you see, not two S'is, that would be more like fussy, and I'm just not fussy at all, oh no, not me, no I am not."

Here Fizzy let out a static little cackle.

"Oh my when I say I'm not fussy I don't mean that about everything you know. I am quite fussy when it comes to man clouds of course. Oh yes, I won't just settle for any old man cloud you know. When I say, 'old man cloud', I don't mean you of course, not that there's anything wrong with you, it's just that I'm a little fussy in that regard you know. And you are a little old, so... Fussy Fizzy, that's me. That's probably why I'm still single of course."

Next Charlie bumped into frothy. Or rather Frothy bumped into Charlie.

"I say old chap, I do 'hic', I do apologuise... 'hic' ...sorry an all."

Frothy was older and rather full-bodied type. A little jaundice maybe, but sporting red, rosy cheeks. Frothy slurred a little and seemed to float to the side, a little off balance.

"A cloud you say?" 'hic' "Very gued... Very good for 'hic' you. I was a cloud once you know. Best 'hic' years of my 'hic' life."

"Um, are you not still a cloud?" Braved Charlie.

"...erm. Shay wat? A cloud you say. Yes. Yes I... Am I?"

Frothy looked down on himself.

"Well I'll 'hic' I'll be damned. You appear to be right Charlie 'hic', Charles old boy. Seems we are both clouds today eh, 'hic'. Well if that doesn't call for a sell...'hic' ...thee... 'hic' ...brat... 'hic' ...tory... 'hic', drink. A shellabratory drink I say! Well then I don't bloody know what does eh, eh. What say you 'hic' Charles old boy. Will you join me for a 'hic' for a jug of the old English?"

Politely Charlie made his excuses and moved on.

Other clouds he met included Pearl, an older lady cloud. Whilst very elegant and attractive, Pearl was also incredibly vain and talked of how she liked to float close to the sea, so that she could catch her and admire her reflection in the waters below. Hard Drive came next. A cloud with a truly encyclopaedic brain. He seemingly knew everything, like all the knowledge on Earth had been stored directly into his cloudy brain. Then came Chilly. Chilly was a musical cloud, able to make notes by freezing moisture to make icicles and blowing on them. Chilly performed for Charlie, leaving him utterly captivated.

Finally, Charlie met Drifter. He was at the back of the pack and appeared to move in continuous circles. Aimless and going nowhere, yet somehow managing to keep up with the pack. He suggested there was a certain beauty in hanging at the back of the pack. No one ever really noticed him. That meant no pressure, which meant he got to study the world going by without any distractions. If it all ever got too much, he could simply drift off undetected and nocloudy would even notice. Charlie couldn't help but feel a little sad for Drifter. He was, though, on board with the logic of what he said. For that reason and no other, Charlie decided to hang at the back of the pack of clouds for a little while. Just drifting and taking it all in.

As Charlie drifted, so too did the pack. They had been following the coastline and now they drifted out to sea over the white cliffs below. Charlie was taken aback by the simple beauty of it all. It felt like, for the first time in his short life, he was finally seeing the beauty of everything that surrounded him. He could feel warmth in the air and smell the salt in the sea. In the distance a hundred hot air balloons floated on a voyage across the channel. Higher up in the sky he felt the hum of a light aircraft speeding by. In his heart he joined in with the laughter of Seagulls, mocking those below that would never know such pleasure.

Charlie's soul now swam with the shadows in the sea and felt a connection to them that, until today, he was unaware even existed. He was all and all were he. He was nothing yet everything he ever wanted to be. He was here, but here was nowhere. Filled up to his top with love and peace, unworried and without a care. In this moment of clarity, he now arrived. On the horizon the Sun began its sleepy descent, and the sky began to fill with glorious colour.

He remembered Ebony. His dear Ebony. As he remembered he realised that this was in fact the second time he had truly felt alive. The first time was the day that they had met. That feeling lasted until the day that they had parted. From that moment, until this, Charlie had been numb and had already been spending his days blocking out the sun. He realised now how futile that life had been and all the time in-between that had been wasted in grief. He thought about her now. He then thought about Lily Cloud and her stories of stars. He decided he would choose to believe that Ebony now resided amongst them.

Had she been looking down on Charlie all this time? If so, what would she have thought of him, wallowing in a pool of self-pity, closed to the wonders of life around him. Could she forgive him, as he was now forced to consider whether he could ever forgive himself. He closed his puffy cloud eyes, offered a silent prayer, to ask for her forgiveness and to hope that she was happy, wherever she was in the Universe. With his eyes closed, and the sound of the sea below, the sky gently swishing, and the birds and the sea, and the sea, and the sky, and th.. and t...

Charlie drifted off, into a most deep and peaceful sleep.

As he slept the pack moved on, the Sun finally set, and Charlie was, once again, left behind in the dark.

Fearing

*'Fear is the path to the Dark Side.
Fear leads to anger, Anger leads
to hate, hate leads to suffering'*
Yoda

BOOM! Flash, flash, cackle...

BOOM! Flash, flash cackle...

BOOM!!!

On the third boom Charlie was jolted back to consciousness.

"What the..? What was that? Where am I?" Charlie desperately asked nobody in particular.

Charlie's first realisation was that he was not, as he usually was, sitting safely in his living room chair. After realising this his second realisation was that he was several thousand feet up in the air. On this second realisation a huge gulf opened within, panic then ambushed, freezing his every sense. Thankfully this second realisation was swiftly followed by a third. That Charlie was now in fact a cloud.

'Phew', he thought to himself. 'For a moment there I thought I was going mad.'

Realisation number three was then followed, as realisations often are, by another. This one that Charlie was on his own, and it was dark.

He stared into the clear skies directly in front of him but found that he could not see Jacob or the rest of the pack. He became aware at the same time of a change in the atmosphere. Something heavy had intruded. Heavy and electric.

BOOM! Flash, flash, cackle cackle...

Charlie turned around to look behind him. The clear dark skies were turning pitch black. The sight was utterly terrifying. This was not one single cloud coming but many. Hundreds. Thousands maybe. Definitely a lot. And these clouds looked much bigger than those Charlie had been floating with before. And they were coming straight at him, fast.

'I have to get out of here,' thought Charlie, and he turned to run. Well, he actually turned to float.

He floated as fast as he could. As fast as the air below would carry him. But he was no match for the approaching mass. Within a minute or two the storm was upon him. At his cloudy toes, then his cloudy knees, then his cloudy waist, then his cloudy neck, then darkness, as the thunderstorm swallowed him whole.

BOOM! Flash, flash, cackle cackle...

In the darkness memories came to Charlie in the flashes. Flash. A memory, then pain, then darkness again. Flash. Another memory, then pain, then darkness again. The memories were of the type best suppressed and hoped forgotten. The type you bury deep, then pile debris high on top, in a bid to keep them in their rightful place, far down and out or range. Out of mind and forgotten. Though those that know also know they can never truly forget. Nothing stays buried forever and the truths that define us, no matter how unpleasant, will eventually rise up and demand to be heard.

BOOM! Flash, flash, cackle cackle...

Memory.

BOOM! Flash, flash, cackle cackle...

Then pain.

BOOM! Flash, flash, cackle cackle...

Memory then pain.

BOOM! Flash, flash, cackle cackle...

Then light.

A circle of sky had opened around Charlie and the painful flashes suddenly ceased. The space remained dark but above Charlie could see the sky again. All around however Charlie was surrounded by very large, thickset, black clouds. These clouds appeared to have electric eyes, all staring now in his direction.

One of the clouds now spoke. A male cloud, with a deep, resonating bass tone that Charlie could feel in his cloud belly.

"Yo whitey. You seem a little lost."

Then he shouted, "BOOM!" Which made Charlie jump inside, and flashed twice

The other clouds around him cackled in appreciation.

"Yeah boy!" Exclaimed the cloud next to him. "You look like you lost yo momma."

BOOM! Flash, flash, cackle, cackle, from the audience.

"In fact, you look a little chubby there boy." This time a lady cloud. "You sure you didn't eat yo momma?"

BOOM! Flash, flash, cackle, cackle...

"Yeah boy." Said the second cloud, now addressing the lady cloud instead of Charlie. "It's a good job he didn't eat your momma. She's so fat she looks like a hippopotamus."

BOOM! Flash, flash, cackle, cackle...

"Ha." Said the lady cloud in response. "Well, yo momma's so fat she looks like a Cumulonimbus."

BOOM!

And this time several other clouds boomed in unison.

Flash, flash, cackle, flash, cackle, cackle, flash flash...

"What you say?" Asked the second cloud, rather angry that he had just been made the butt of the joke. "You wanna talk about mommas? At least I got a momma. You so ugly yo momma abandoned you. I know 'cus she told me so last night when I was..."

Here the lady cloud swelled to twice the size and let out an almighty BOOOOOM! At the same time, she shot a bolt of lightning that fired through the clouds all the way down to the ground below.

"What you wanna say about my momma?" She shouted.

"Okay, okay." Said the first cloud. "Cool it there lady. You're scaring our guest. Young whitey here is looking a little pale."

BOOM! Flash, flash, cackle cackle...

Charlie was scared, at first. But now, having listened to the interactions around him, he felt the need to speak. So, he piped up.

"Um, excuse me," he said. "But who are you all and what do you people want with me?"

"Ha." Reacted one, who seemed to be the head cloud. "Will ya look at that. Little whitey here has found his voice. What was that you said my friend? What do we want with you? What do we want with you? Ha, you got some grit I give you that. The question is what do you want with us? You came into our territory dude, not the other way around. Oh, an by the way, we ain't people, we are clouds. Not just any old clouds either, but 'Thee Clouds', you dig? THUNDER CLOUDS!" He roared.

'BOOM,' 'BOOM,' 'BOOM,' from all around they came.

After all the 'booming' had calmed down, Charlie put forward another question. "What do you mean when you say territory? Last time I checked this was called 'the sky.' I don't recall anyone as owning the sky."

"Ha." Replied the main man cloud. "You sure about that whitey? You sure you got your facts straight there little cloud? What's wrong, yo momma never tell you about the birds and the bees? How about the wind in the trees? How about the sun always setting in the west? An how about how that thunderclouds is the best? You may have been a land walker once my friend, but now you in the sky with me. An guess what, little white cloud, you are in my territory 'cus my territory is wherever I am? So, I ask you again my friend, what is it you want, 'cus there ain't no little white cloud ever been brave enough to wander into my hood in all the years I been a thundercloud. So spill it boy."

BOOM, flash flash, cackle, cackle.

"Well." Started Charlie. "First of all, there is nothing that I want from you. I didn't float here by choice. I was travelling with a pack of very nice clouds but happened to drift off. And well, when I came to you were already approaching and I, well I, appear to have rather lost the clouds that I was travelling with. They were white clouds by the way, and generally very pleasant."

"You saying black clouds ain't pleasant whitey?"

"No, no. That's not at all what I am saying. And in fact I think you are being a little bit racist, if I may say so, by keep referring to me as whitey."

"Oh, okay. So, first time you ever meet a bunch of black clouds the best you can imagine is them playing dozens, throwing 'yo momma' snaps at each other. An' you think I'm being racist?"

"Well, no, fair. But I mean... Well, what I was trying to get at is... Well, what is the difference between black and white clouds anyway?"

"Well that might be the first sensible question you have asked since you have been here. There may be hope for you after all."

"Yeah boy." Chipped in the second cloud. "There ain't no difference between us white and black clouds."

"Except," said the third cloud, "that we make these cotton wool suits look good."

Boom, flash flash, cackle cackle.

"Yeah boy." Exclaimed the second cloud again. "We might wear these suits better than you, but we all silver on the inside brother."

"And just how do you know that?" Questioned the third cloud. "I'm damn sure you ain't ever seen my lining?"

"No." Said the second cloud in agreement. "Maybe not your lining, but I have seen yo momma's and she has the shiniest lin..."

BOOOOOOMMMM!!!

The third cloud was at it again and threw another thunderbolt groundward.

"Will you stop being so rude to her about her mother please?" Charlie demanded of the second cloud.

This stunned the second cloud into a shocked silence, from which he was about to reply when cloud number three, now back to her normal size, piped up.

"Hey whitey, that takes some guts to speak up to one of us thunderclouds. Looks like you are alright my man, and you know how to treat a lady. Thank you."

"You are welcome." Said Charlie.

"So, what name do you go by then? Other than whitey that is?"

"Charlie." Stated Charlie. "Charlie Thatcher is my name."

"Well pleased to meet you, Charlie. My name is Patricia. Or 'Lady Rage', as I am sometimes called by these fellas. This sorry excuse for a thundercloud is called Diesel. He's been busy polluting the sky with his poor excuses for humour for some time now. And this man here is the boss. The legendary Grand Master."

"Now hold it, Lady Rage." Replied Grand Master (GM for short). "You know I don't buy into that legendary nonsense."

"But it's true. And young Charlie here, well he should know that he is in the presence of greatness. This cloud here Charlie is a pioneer. Before GM all the Thunderclouds in the sky... Well, they knew how to boom and flash, and cackle and cackle, but they had no style you know. They would start up one type of storm, then flip into another completely different storm altogether. The GM here showed them how to work together, you know, to work in unison. To shape, to build, to define. To find the rhythm and keep the storm going. Man, we have only had the best of times since then."

"Wow." Said Charlie, impressed.

"Yes." Replied the GM. "Rage speaks the truth and we have indeed had the best of times. The work has taken me to every town in every country. But enough. Enough about me. We need to speak about you and figure out why you have come among us."

"Well, maybe..." Suggested Charlie quite brightly. "Maybe it is so I can be a thundercloud like you?"

At that the whole audience bounced about with laughter.

BOOM, BOOM, BOOM, flash, cackle, flash, flash, cackle boom...

"That, my brother, might be just about the funniest thing I have ever heard."

Charlie The Thundercloud

When the laughter and general merriment of the thunderclouds had eventually subsided Charlie, now feeling rather put out, questioned the GM as to why he could not be a thundercloud. The GM explained that to produce a bolt of thunder the host cloud needed to possess a certain amount of rage. Rage born of anger. To be an effective thundercloud the possessor had to possess a certain amount of control over that rage. It was no good just firing off thunderbolts left right and middle. Who knows what or who might get hit. The GM also explained what the thunderclouds were and their reason for being.

The storms they created were not there to cause chaos, though it is true that some humans might disagree when a storm affected their human worlds. Storms instead were there to clear the airs, from whatever negativity and pollutants they had amassed. Their bolts of lightning were not a tool to generate fear but designed to offer energy and light into the darkness. Their thunder, not a sound of attack but of jubilation. Cleansing, energising, lighting, and dancing up the sky. Then, when the storms were done, they would clear the way and let the more gentle rain clouds take over and wash everything clean. Charlie very much liked the sound of this and asked the GM again if he could not be a thundercloud.

"Well, Charlie my cloud, why don't we just try and see how you get on eh? Before anything else we gotta find out what makes you angry. So, what makes you angry Charlie?"

"Well..." mused Charlie. "I don't very much like listening to the news. Specifically, I don't like lying politicians, which is most politicians. You know, I have heard it said that anyone wishing to have a career in politics should be banned from being a politician. I think that is a good idea. That way more honest folk may have a chance at running things. And lord knows they could do no worse. I mean, what is wrong with just giving a straight answer to a straight question. Ggrrr, those Weasley snakes make me so cross."

And the GM did observe this to be true. Politicians did indeed make Charlie angry for his form had swelled just a little, and his white exterior now took on a more grey, ashen look.

"Okay Charlie, this is good. I can see you don't like them dudes that run things. But they ain't gonna do it I'm afraid. We gonna need to dig a little deeper. Think now, what or who makes you really angry?"

"Well, that's a thing you see. I don't really know any people anymore. There is a young girl at the chip shop I suppose. Though I don't suppose she knows my name and I certainly don't know hers."

"There has to be someone Charlie. What about all the people in your street? I mean, don't you know any of them?"

"No!" Charlie snapped. "I don't know them, and they don't care to know me. In fact, it is them that started this whole sorry business of me floating around in the sky like I haven't got a care. I mean, when I go out, I just want to mind my own business and I want them to mind theirs. But oh no. Stare at me they do. Judge me they do. Cast assertions in their minds and talk about me behind my back. I know they do, and I hate them for it."

Charlie was starting to change appearance now. He had swelled to at least twice the size and was now presenting more of a charcoal appearance, no longer pristine white.

"That's it Charlie boy." Encouraged the GM. "Keep talking about how you hate 'em. I can see the anger is in you after all. Tell me more."

"Well, I just hate them is all. I hate the way they are all so happy and..." At this point Charlie's voice began to trail off. "I am not... I am not happy." It was like this was the first time in all these years that Charlie had realised this out loud. The fact that he did not hate them, for they had never done anything unto him for him to hate. Not really. He decided they hated him because it was easier than accepting, he was not happy because of his own choices. Because he had chosen to be alone. As Charlie had this realisation he began to shrink back. Back to his normal small size. The whiteness returned as his anger dissipated into the air around him. With the realisation came a change of direction in the wind. Charlie didn't notice that the wind had changed. However, slowly but surely, Charlie and the thunderclouds started to drift their way back toward the land. Back in the direction they had come. Back toward the street where Charlie lived and the house in which he existed.

"Charlie Charlie Charlie." Exclaimed the GM with a sigh. "You were doing so well."

"Maybe you were right." Charlie conceded. "Maybe I am not cut out for this thundercloud thing after all."

"No man." Replied the GM. "You have the anger in you Charlie boy. I can see it. You just haven't gotten to its true source yet. Come on now. Let us dig real deep. Deeper than you have ever been before. Who was it Charlie? Come on. Who was it that made you hurt so? And why have you never been properly mad about it?"

Charlie knew of course. He had always known. There was only one real person who had ever really hurt Charlie. He had buried it though. Buried it deep, deep inside. Deeper than he ever thought was possible. Deeper than any other feeling he had ever had. Buried it and filled in the hole with concrete. Then built a fortress upon it, fortified with an elite guard. No human being was ever going to get to these feelings but the GM, of course, was not a human being. As the GM began to probe the guards began to scatter and the ground began to shake. The fortress turned to rubble and the concrete cracked. The ground now rumbled, bubbled, shook violently as the buried thing beneath now demanded resurrection.

It wasn't her fault. He knew this. Of course, he knew this. She would never have chosen to leave, but she had left him all the same. Gone, in the blink of a tear drenched eye. Gone, and left him to face the world alone. Gone, and left him to walk the streets alone. Gone, and left him to eat his meals alone. Gone, and left him to watch TV and listen to the radio on his own. Gone, and left him to do it all, to do it all on his own. Everything now, alone.

"I mean." Charlie suddenly said aloud. "How was I supposed to enjoy the sunshine after you left me?"

Charlie began to grow.

'How was I supposed to sit and watch a sunset knowing you weren't there at the end of it?"

Charlie grew darker.

"How was I supposed to care what clothes to wear? Who was I wearing them for?"

"That's it Charlie boy. Whatever you are thinking, keep it up."

"How was I supposed to face our friends again, after you left me?"

Charlie was louder now, starting to shout. Growing bigger, growing darker.

"How was I supposed to go out? To watch a show, to have a drink, to take a walk, to have fun. How was I supposed to have fun after you damn well went and left me damn it?"

Sparks were flying now within Charlie's chest, and he was suddenly almost equal in size to the GM.

"How the hell was I supposed to walk down the street again, after they all knew that I lost you?

After they all knew that you both left me. Grrrrr..." Charlie growled and let out a cry of rage toward the street. 'BOOM!' And so, a thunderbolt sprang forth from Charlie and drove into the ground, scorching the street below.

"There you go!" Chimed the GM. "Now you're doing it."

"Stupid bloody street. Stupid bloody street and all the stupid bloody people in it."

Charlie grew again, now becoming bigger than the GM, and darker too.

BOOM! BOOM! BOOM!

Charlie sent three fresh bolts down into the street below. One hit and scorched the road. Another hit and severed a tree branch. The third took out a street sign. People down below, those still left on the streets, started to panic and scatter and run for shelter.

"Whoa there Charlie boy! Take it easy man. A true thundercloud needs to be able to control their bolts and..."

But Charlie wasn't listening anymore. Led by a feeling of pure rage and power Charlie was not going to stop now. He could not remember ever feeling angry like this. Angry, yet mighty at the same time.

BOOM! BOOM! BOOM!

Three more bolts fired into the street below.

"Ha ha ha... That's right. You're not laughing now are you?"

BOOM!

"Or talking behind my back."

BOOM!'

"Or feeling sorry for me. Not anymore. Not now."

BOOM! BOOM! BOOM!

"COME ON THEN!"

"Yo Charlie cloud." The GM, shouting now. "You gotta stop this man. Chill your boots..."

But Charlie still wasn't listening. It was then that Charlie spotted his house. His house. His home. 'Pah.' His prison is more like. That empty, stinking, rotten, foetid shell that weighed him down, held him down, kept him cold and alone and out of sight and out of mind. In recognising his house Charlie swelled in size again. Now monolithic in size and darker than a piece of coal, wrapped in black cloth, hidden in a blacked-out room, in a darkened building, in the middle of a dark black night. Charlie was massive. Charlie was beautiful. Charlie was on fire.

"That house. That stupid house. THAT STUPID BLOODY HOUSE!"

Charlie sent a massive thunderbolt hurtling toward the roof.

BOOOOM!!!

Tiles were sent flying and a massive hole appeared, revealing the space within the loft. At this Charlie remembered all the boxed memories that they had kept there. Photos of those good times, when they were younger, when they were happy. Boxes of keepsakes. Letters written to each other. Postcards and ticket stubs, programmes, newspaper clippings. Teddy bears, mementos, talismans, all from happier times. All personal to them. Now only personal to him. Who the hell was going to miss them when Charlie was gone?

"GGGGGRRRRR..."

BBBOOOOMMM!

This next thunderbolt took the roof right off, scattering debris everywhere.

Memories now afloat and on fire, lifted into the air, ready to scatter as ashen confetti onto the streets below. The bedroom was revealed now.

The place where they used to lay, together. Lazy Sunday mornings spent reading the papers. Cuddles in the dark, giggles in the light. Safe, warm, and secure, in the middle of the night. Charlie could not bear to see.

BBBOOOOOMMMM!
BBBOOOOOOOMMMM!
BBBOOOOOOOOMMMM!

The GM and the other thunderclouds had since backed off. They had never seen the like before. It was clear that the GM had created a monster that was now off its leash and out of control.

Meanwhile Charlie could now see into the living room. Or should that be '...the dying room?' For there was no more living to be done there since she'd left him. He looked at the old TV. He looked at the tired old dining table. He focused on the chair where he now spent his endless days. At this point a rage, so absolute, so primal, so complete, so all consuming, so righteous and pure, completely overwhelmed him. He drew in a massive breath, for what felt like an age. People below struggled to catch their breath as the oxygen seemed momentarily disappeared. He held it in. He held it down. Held it and held it until it began to hurt. And then...

Charlie let it out with everything he had.

A massive thunderbolt of pure white light was released that lit up the whole night sky.

BBBBBBBOOOOOOOOOOMMMMMM!!!!!!

The resulting light and sound would be spoken of by the humans for many years to come, witnessed as it was for miles and miles around.

This final bolt was sent crashing into Charlie's chair. Into that dying room. Into what remained of that house.

That home.

That prison.

Charlie was spent, and so now, was his house.

Charlie began to shrink.

Whilst deflating Charlie spotted a solitary piece of paper floating in the air, within the debris, above the wreckage, that was once his house. Carried into the sky by the force of the final blast, suspense sustained by the heat from the fires below. It was soon close enough for Charlie to recognise. It was a photograph. Not just any photograph, this was the photograph. The one of Ebony and Charlie that had sat upon the TV. The one that Charlie had gazed at for hours upon end every single day. It was her. It was his final memory of her. As Charlie thought to reach out the photo began to fall, back toward the ground, back toward the wreckage and back toward the fires. All too soon the photo was lost to the flames, along with everything else.

'What have I done?' Thought Charlie. 'Oh my. What have I done?'

At this point the numbness began to seep in. A stale, all consuming, catatonic, cold, crystallising numbness, dulling every sense, choking every pore.

The GM was alongside him now, talking, or shouting even. He couldn't be sure. He saw gestures. The cloud lips moved but he could not hear what they were saying.

"Charlie dude. Those were some seriously messed up moves. What were you thinking?"

Charlie looked down at himself and noticed he was not reverting to white, but rather he was turning a dirty grey.

"I mean, listen. It's clear that you ain't no thundercloud after all. You can't just go around blowing up stuff like that."

Charlie was starting to have the sensation of weight.

"Look, it ain't nothing personal my friend but you can't roll with us no more. You hear what I'm saying Charlie? We got a rep. Charlie, do you hear me?"

A ringing, buzzing noise started to sound in Charlie's mind. The weight was increasing. He was numb but was starting to feel like he might be sick.

"Charlie. I've arranged for my friend here to take you to see some clouds you may be better suited to. Other clouds that couldn't cut it as thunder clouds you know. But listen, it ain't nothing personal and it ain't nothing to be ashamed of. Not all of us are cut out for the top you know. And anyway..."

GM's cloud lips continued to move, and the GM continued to make gestures. A small cloud had appeared at Charlie's side, somehow familiar. The small cloud gestured him forwards, took a hold of him and suddenly, just like that, Charlie was on the move.

Suffering

'People are like stained glass windows. They sparkle & shine when the sun is out, but when the darkness sets in, their true beauty is revealed only if there is a light from within' Elisabeth Kubler-Ross

He suddenly realised he was not with the GM anymore. He then realised that he was moving. He was not in control of where though and the scenery seemed to rush past him like it were being projected onto a background screen in a static movie set. He felt heavy, bloated and quite sick. Being sick wasn't one of the things he liked to do though, so he fought hard to suppress this.

As he further came round, he started to notice distant sounds of what sounded like sobbing. Looking down at himself he noticed he had become rather thick-set and dirty grey in colour. The space around him was turning the same grey in colour and he was feeling heavier by the minute. The sobbing sounds grew louder and the sky about him grew greyer and he was growing heavier and everything, everything, was closing in. He felt panic rise, then fear. He was suddenly very afraid and now feeling very very sick. The fear he felt was not like that when he had seen the advance of the thunderclouds. No, this fear was something deeper. More primal and far more terrifying. He knew something was coming for him, from him, and he did not believe himself to be ready.

The sobbing sounds were intense now. Louder and coming from all around him. Voices now overlaid, punctuating the sobs.

"Let us in. Let us in. Let us in." The demand being repeated over and over in low moans.

"Charlie. Charlie. Charlie! Listen, you must stay close to me now, just like I said, remember?"

He could not remember.

"Where, where are we?" He spluttered weakly.

"We are with the rainclouds, remember?"

"But what, who... What are all these clouds here?"

He could feel them now. Individual clouds pressing against him, pressing into him. Gripping him. Trying to consume him into their collective mass.

'Oh my,' he thought. 'These clouds are actually trying to eat me!'

"Help!" To no one in particular he let out a terrified yell. "Help me. These clouds are trying to eat me."

"Just keep moving. Like I told you, eyes down and stay close."

Together they pushed on, into the throbbing heart and heat of the grotesque mass.

"Keep moving and they won't be able to take you."

He found new strength in his fear and pushed on with his guide. This despite feeling like an overinflated waterbed, bloated on fear and panic, with a sickness he did not yet understand.

The sobbing had grown so loud now that it was all he could clearly hear. Sobbing, crushing, and moaning.

"LET US IN. LET US IN. LET US IN. LET US..."

xx lol xx

All at once he felt himself being pulled, through an invisible barrier, and all the sobbing and moaning noise suddenly stopped. A new sound now, like what one might observe if listening to a running shower from an adjoining room. The space he now found himself in was cavernous and vast. Dark and grey, like an abandoned warehouse. Moulded skylights were positioned high up in the ceiling. Enough light to sense but not enough to illuminate. The space stretched on for as far as he could make out. Both in front and to the sides.

 Within the space was row upon row of slightly raised, dark, rectangle spaces. The spaces were positioned close to one another, with each sporting its own stubby headboard. Raised only a couple of inches above the ground but like icebergs, each was sunken, a further six feet into the floor. His first thought was of a hospital ward. A huge continuous ward, with no doors, no pillars, no noisy machines. No smell of hospital food or bodily fluids or of orange squashes or hand sanitizers or disinfectant. His second thought was of somewhere far more sinister. In the air hung an appropriate atmosphere of grief, loss, soon to be lost, hope and hopelessness. Then he was reminded of his nausea as a fresh wave crashed into his shore and almost overcame him.

In a strained voice he asked. "What is this place? Is this a cloud hospital? Am I sick? Is this why you have brought me here? I do feel a bit sick." And by a bit sick he meant really sick.

"Well, it's not really a hospital. Though it kind of is too I suppose. We are in the heart of a giant storm. A giant rainstorm made up of so many clouds. Within each of these pods you can see is a single cloud. Burdened with weight but now letting go of its load."

"And the clouds outside?"

"They are all rain clouds. They are all sick with sadness of some sort. They fight to get into the heart so that they might use one of these pods, where they will in turn be relieved of their load and thus renewed."

"Well why not let them in then? I mean, why make them suffer outside."

"Alas, there are only so many pods. The great cloud council has practised austerity now over many years. There has been little new investment into the rain cloud system and I'm afraid admittance is now made on a case-by-case basis, judged on a case's severity."

"Oh, I see. Um, well how did we get in then if..?"

Before he had finished the question, he already knew the answer.

"Oh. I'm really sick, aren't I?"

"Yes. I'm afraid you really are."

"Ah..."

"But do not fear. A pod has been reserved and you will be feeling right as rain in no time, so to speak."

With that he was led through the endless rows of pods, deeper into the storm. Passing by the pods he noticed that scenes seemed to play out upon their transparent surfaces. Each looked like a scene from an old technicolour movie show.

"What are they?" He asked.

"They are the stories. The things that the clouds have witnessed. The things that have led to the clouds being here. They are recalled and played out within the pods, so that the cloud may process them then let them go. Thus, releasing the burden."

"I'm not sure I understand."

"Well, a cloud sees many things of this world, and many of the things a cloud sees are very sad. Too sad for words. For every sadness a tear must be shed, for that is the nature of such things. In order to retain a cosmic balance, you see."

"Um, okay. I think I understand that. But there are so many clouds here. Surely enough tears are shed by humans?"

"Well, it turns out that it takes a lot to make a human sad these days. Or certainly a lot to make a human cry. To maintain balance, there is no choice for these clouds but to soak up the excess sadness and cry on the humans' behalf. That is why there are so many clouds here now. That is also why there is so much water in the world and that the sea levels are rising. A cloud cries a hundred times more tears than that of a human. A hundred and one times more when the human does not cry at all. Arrogance, pride, or denial stop humans from seeing, accepting, and letting in what is in front of them, holding back the tears. Desensitisation through media exposure stops the rest. Besides, there is no time for tears when there is fun to be had and money to be made. What's more, the size of this storm cloud alone could easily lead to a flooding event, which in turn could lead to some new human tragedy, which in turn would lead to more pent-up anguish for which not nearly enough human tears would be shed. The more tragedy that humans see, the colder their hearts become. The colder their hearts become, the more tears the clouds must release on their behalf. The more tears that the clouds must cry, the more tragedy the humans will see. Why don't you look at some of the pods for yourself."

Doubled over with sickness, he floated to the nearest pod. Here he witnessed images of a ruined city. Nothing now but rubble and broken buildings. Conscripted ashen faced soldiers, forced into someone else's fight. Regular soldiers, whose time had finally come, displaying a certain delight. Missiles, tanks, bombs, and guns. Bodies strewn about the place. Civilians on the run. The horror of war, in all its pointless glory, where all can only lose.

He moved on to another story.

Here he saw a small boat, caught out in the sea. A raft meant for rescue, designed for lives to be saved, here so overcrowded, sailing them instead to graves. Those adults that were huddled were desperate but held down their fears for the sake of the children on board. They were caught in a storm. They were trapped in a small boat on a big sea. No one was coming for them. Everybody knew that they were not supposed to be there.

He moved on to the next pod.

Human men, eight to a room, thirty-two to the house. A house, toxic with damp, mould and sweat. Leaking taps, broken boiler, draughty steamed windows. They fought so hard to get here. Now, with documents in the charge of their beneficiaries, they want nothing more than to leave, but cannot.

He moved on again.

A killer in a school with a gun. A child killer of other children. As prey, the other children now dispersed in fear, suddenly a part of this fatal lottery.

He moved on.

A motor car rests broken; innocent young lives lost. Other drivers are frustrated and angry to be caught up in the resulting traffic delays.

He moves on.

Children put to work here. Poor conditions, no rights, no pay.

He move on...

Forests stripped naked and bare for financial gain.

He moved...

Animals burning as they futilely flee from forest fires.

He moves...

Earth toxified as the gluttony of humanity races to consume the next consumable thing whilst discarding the last. Landfills filling, resources dwindling, economy growing. Mother Earth choking.

He moo...

The sickness. The madness. The insanity surges up in him now.

His mind splits with migraine. His eyes can no longer focus.

His whole being is desperately trying to force his sickness out.

Still, he refuses to let it go.

"Come!" Said now with urgency. "We must get you to your pod!"

Dragging himself he follows, as they move amongst the seemingly endless corridors between the pods. Finally, they came upon an empty pod. Like all the others, only this one is bright and not dark. This one is empty. This one is for him.

"Right. We are here."

Shallow breaths, unsure of what to do.

"What am I supposed to do?" He asks, desperation clear in his voice.

"Just get into the pod. Now. The storm will take care of the rest."

He struggles to raise and pull himself over the lip of the pod. He is assisted with a firm push. He has never felt this heavy before nor has he ever felt this sick. He makes it over the edge and into the pod with a flop. He looks back at his guide through crackled eyes.

"Wait a minute. You're Jacob, aren't you?"

Jacob has no time for a proper reply. Immediately a film lid started to close over the pod.

Suddenly he panics and cries out.

"Jacob, what is going to happen to you?"

"Do not worry about me. I will be right here. Do not fear. I shall not leave you alone. I will be with you every float of the way."

The film lid then seals shut, and he is alone.

Alone in the pod and the darkness now returned.

For what seems like an age he lays, alone in that darkness. He groans and the unbearable sickness continues to force at his borders, but still he refuses to let it go. A new voice comes to him now. Warm, knowing, and caring. A voice, female and instantly recognisable. It is just as he remembers, from all those years ago, when they were still young. Young and in love. The voice is of course Ebony.

Releasing

'How lucky I am to have something that makes saying goodbye so hard.' Winnie the Pooh

The darkness dispersed. Charlie began to recognise his surroundings. Charlie was back in his living room. His living room, it may have been, but it was somehow different now. Everything was fresh and clean and light. Charlie found himself reclined on his couch. He was himself again. The same but somehow different. He noticed his favourite brown brogues at the end of his legs. He became aware of music playing in the background. He spotted two crystal tumblers perched on the table, each sporting a fine single malt whiskey. Then he looked up and he saw her. Her. Ebony. She was sitting there, right there, with him, at the end of the couch.

"But, but... How can it be? Ebony. Is that really you?"

"Why Charlie, of course it's me. Who else would it be?"

"But I... But you... I mean you... I mean, well... I have had the strangest dream. I've had a few strange dreams come to think of it. I dreamt that you left me, and that I got old, and that I lived alone, and then we caught a cloud, and then I became a cloud and, and... Well, it all seemed very real. I mean... Wow!"

Letting out a big sigh, the epic sense of relief that Charlie now felt was immense. Thank goodness. It was all just a horrible, horrible dream and now, at last, he was awake again.

The feeling though was not to last. Ebony, his beautiful Ebony, looked him in the eye. She raised her hand, placing it against the side of his face. Tender, warm, familiar.

"Charlie. I'm afraid you weren't dreaming. What has happened to you is real. All of it. I'm afraid I really did leave you and I am so, so sorry for that. But it was my time and I had to go."

The sickness that Charlie had been feeling previously now returned with full force. Letting out a yelp he doubled over, pain flooding into every atom of his being. He caught his breath, forcing some composure.

"But I don't understand. If you really did leave me, what are you doing here? How can I be talking to you now? I... I don't understand. And I don't feel very well. Oh my, I think I am going to be sick."

Again, he put all his focus into holding back the sickness.

"Charlie. Stop fighting it."

"Stop fighting what?"

"Stop fighting the pain, Charlie. You need to let it go. That is why I am here now and that is what I have come to tell you. It's time Charlie. You need to let go now. You need to let me go."

"But I can't. I mean I won't. I... Arrrghhh... I..."

Charlie fell to the floor and doubled up into the foetal position. His eyes scrunched shut in pain and he held himself.

Ebony knelt beside him and began to stroke his hair.

"It's okay Charlie. Let it go. Just let go."

At this Charlie felt something dislodge inside of him. A tiny movement at first, but of something large. Rain started to tip tap gently against the windowpane. Ebony looked to the windowpane, then looked back at Charlie.

"That's it Charlie, that's the way. Let it go now. Let Me Go."

The gentle tapping increased in frequency.

"That's it Charlie."

Charlie was able to open his eyes. Was it his imagination or was Ebony now starting to glow?

"Keep going Charlie. Just let go. That's all you must do."

The rain was getting much harder now and the tip tap, tip tap turned into a drumbeat. Charlie felt himself relax a little and unfold, the sickness starting to subside. But the guilt. How could he let Ebony go? How could he let Ebony go like he had let her go. He wanted to be in pain, he deserved to be in pain. But now he was finally letting it go, after all these years, and Ebony was glowing more, definitely glowing, and getting brighter by the second.

The thing that shifted inside of him moved more now. He could feel the pressure growing. The power of all the Earth's oceans pushing against a single cork in a bottle. This flood could not be held back any longer.

BANG! It came. The cork finally gave way.

All the seas were now forcing their way out. Freed at last from their confinement. The sickness, no longer pain but relief. He felt the saliva in his mouth and the air in his lungs. All the colours changed, and the world was rearranged. The lights were flickering back on and a darkness he did not even know was there began to subside. The oxygen came rushing in and his vision began to clear.

He looked at her now. Ebony. He knew that this would be the last time. The last time at least in this life that he would be able to look upon the person he adored the most. A bright, soft white light shone all around her and she was smiling. The kind of smile that lights up a room. No. The kind of smile that lights up a house. No. The kind of a smile that lights up a whole life. And it had.

The rain beat so hard now that the pane in the window shattered and the curtains in the room came alive. Wind, rain, and noise filled the room. The pain, the relief from the pain, the oxygen, the colours, the ethereal glow from his Ebony was sending him dizzy and he could feel things now slipping away from him.

"Thank you, Charlie. Thank you. I will see you again soon. Very soon."

At this Ebony began to fade into the light. Into the warmth. Into the past.

The brightness became all consuming. A pure, surreal white light. Charlie was consumed and felt nothing but pure love. He knew at that moment that everything was going to be okay.

Blowing Out the Flame

Suddenly the scenery changed again, and Charlie found himself back in the pod, back in the rain cloud. With his head back in the clouds he felt his body starting to slide. He was sliding from the base of the cloud.

He looked down and he could now see legs. Actual legs. His legs. They were dangling from the base of the rainstorm cloud. He could feel himself slipping further. Below his feet he could see the

Earth. A long, long way down but it was there for sure. The rain was thundering now, and Charlie was sliding further downwards with the heavy drops. Summoned by gravity from the safety of the pod he realised he felt no fear.

A torso now. His torso. Somewhere in his mind he was aware also of his arms and his hands that were now gripping subconsciously to the inside of the pod.

"Just let go Charlie."

Ebony's words echoed in his ears.

"Just let go."

So he did.

Falling

'You drown not by falling into a river, but by staying submerged in it' Paulo Coelho

Heavy but weightless, falling but rising. Charlie was moving fast on his way down now, though his spirit was coming up. Spread out like a starfish he could see far below where the land met the sea, or where the sea met the land. Whatever. He knew now that both were the same thing. One simply a continuation of the other, just in a different form. Part of the same. Part of the same whole. He also knew that where the land ended, and the sea began there would be a divide. Rocky, sharp, hostile, and final. He knew that this was where he was heading now.

The sounds about him had changed. The rushing wind raged past his ears, creating a new kind of silence in which he could meditate. Charlie turned in the air, rolled onto his back, and looked up instead, to the dark clouds above. He could feel the rain falling with him and onto his face, washing away the last of residues of fears that had crippled him for so long.

As he fell his mind reflected. He thought back to the life that he had lived and of the lessons he felt he had learnt. Everything was so clear to Charlie now it was like a new, bright, all-encompassing light had been switched on. Every dark corner, every small crevice, every valley, every groove lay revealed. The entire cosmos and every mystery within it now finally came into view. At once he knew everything and realised, he had known nothing.

He knew now that everything was, and always had been, okay.

The black
The white
The shapes
The rocks
The loneliness
The happiness.
The fear
The lack of confidence
The self-doubt
The music
The maths
The dreams
The losses
The imaginations
The disappointments
The diseases
The cures
The wars
The new age healings
The pharmaceuticals
To live without purpose
To be irrelevant
To be without meaning
To be every soul that had ever existed

He understood now how the whole thing was deceiving. Everything mattered, but nothing he did mattered.

He could feel the true love now, the illusion was shattered.

It was time.

It was his time.

Time to go.

Completely overwhelmed, peace was all he could feel as the jagged rocks rushed up beneath him to break his fall.

It was time to go.

He closed his eyes, spread out his arms and waited for impact.

Finally, he had truly let go.

'Poof.'

The flame expired.

Then 'VOOMP..!'

Charlie had landed.

Ending

'Everything will be okay in the end. If it's not okay, it's not the end" John Lennon

'Well, that was odd.'

The rushing sounds had ceased. Charlie was no longer falling. He hadn't felt any pain like he had expected. He did not feel broken and scattered, as he thought that he might by now. Nor spattered and gooey, the remnants of a man shaped water bomb. Instead, he had felt the most incredible softness and warmth. An all-encompassing embrace, a loving cuddle if you will. A soft warm bed. It was like he had landed not onto rocks, but onto a....

'Wait a minute.'

He dared not think it, but it was as though he had landed on a...

It was like he had been caught by a...

'Caught by a CLOUD!'

"Charlie?" Questioned a now familiar voice.

"Charlie." The voice said again, though this time more pressing.

"Open your eyes, Charlie. Charlie. Open your eyes."

Charlie obliged and slowly he opened his eyes.

"Jacob!" He exclaimed. "What... What on earth are you doing here? I don't understand."

Jacob smiled. "I imagine it has all been very confusing. Let me help you, Charlie. Let me help you understand. When you are ready, I want you to look down."

Charlie looked down.

What Charlie saw knocked the wind out of him. For a second he thought he was going to panic and hyperventilate. As soon as that feeling came though it went away and was replaced, again, with a surreal sense of calm and goodness. A tear did form though, at the corner of Charlie's right eye.

Charlie had the urge to say aloud that he didn't understand, but of course he did. He did understand. He. He, Charlie. Charlie Thatcher. Charlie Thatcher the cloud catcher was there, slumped there below him, lifeless and still. Unaware was his old friend now. With eyes forever closed. Charlie was dead and now Charlie knew. With all the clarity in the universe he now knew. He had passed and now he knew that he had passed. But still he felt the need to ask the question to Jacob. As if hearing it played back would make it become more real.

"Jacob? Am I... Am I dead?"

"Well Charlie, let's instead say that you have passed."

"But I still don't understand. I was at the house with you. I caught you and I took you back to the house. In fact, I destroyed that house. I destroyed everything after I became a cloud like you. How can I be here? How can you be here? I was falling and, and..."

"You were falling, Charlie. Yes, you were. And I caught you, Charlie. I caught you and I got you."

"But... But I was a cloud. I was like you. I was a cloud just like you."

"Well..."

"But I... I caught you, remember? I caught you in my net in the monkey castle. Me and Ebony and Sid, we caught you."

"No Charlie, you didn't. I only let you think you did. You see Charlie, you didn't catch me, Charlie. I caught you."

"But I... But you... But... Wait a minute. Are you even a real cloud?"

"Charlie, you were dying. You were dying but you were not ready to accept it and move on. My job Charlie, my role if you will, is to assist lost souls. Souls just like you. I help them with... Well, I help them with their transition. To the other side, as you humans like to call it. You might prefer to think of me as an Angel. I only appeared as a cloud as that is what was right for you."

"You mean I've been dead all this time? None of this was real?"

"It was all real Charlie, and you were alive, but you were also dying. You were dying and you were lost. But I found you. You thought you found me, but I found you. You thought you caught me Charlie, but it was always my job to catch you."

The tear that had formed in the corner of his right eye was now set free. Charlie felt it roll, then streak down his face, then drop from his chin. This would be Charlie's last ever tear.

"It is time for you to leave now Charlie. I am here to show you the final stretch of the way back home. When you are ready, I would like you to follow me."

Charlie was ready. He thought he was ready a long time ago but now he was truly ready. He was ready to go now. To go back home.

"Come now Charlie. Say your goodbyes and follow me."

Taking one last look. One last deep long look at himself, or rather the self he used to be, he whispered, "...goodbye Charlie. Thank you for having me. It was... It was fun."

Charlie's Final Act

He followed Jacob, up into the sky. Clouds once more, but different this time. Lighter. Freer. Together they rose, together they flew. Swifter than birds, faster than jet places. Souls that had been set free, with no weights to slow them down. Like dreams coming true they rose and flew. Up, up, higher, and higher, until they were there, at the edge of time and space itself.

"Well Charlie, this is me. You need to travel the rest of the way by yourself."

"You mean you're not coming with me?"

"Ha, I wish. Some of us still have jobs to do. Besides, you won't want me cramping your style when you are with Ebony"

Charlie had a feeling, like a heart racing, at the sound of Ebony's name.

He looked up and could see not a sky, but a Universe. A whole Universe full of stars.

"Wow! Does this mean it is real? We really do go back to the stars?"

"Yes Charlie, it is real, and it is time now for you to take your place back amongst them. Ebony is waiting for you."

"But how do I know? How do I know which star is Ebony?"

Jacob gave a hearty laugh.

"Oh Charlie, have you not learnt anything? Simply look for the one that shines the brightest."

With that Charlie said his final goodbye, moved on from our world and went home.

Charlie went home.

Epilogue

Forgotten

*'Death does not concern us,
because as long as we exist,
death is not here. And when it
does come, we no longer exist'*
Epicurus

Detective Orwell (49) and Detective Huxley (32) were in attendance at the scene of the crime. The police had taped off the area that morning and the detectives were now sitting on a bench, coffees in hand, reviewing the evidence and notes that they had collated thus far.

The pair had initially spoken with Lily, who was a server at the coffee shack, located at the centre of the park, close to where they now sat. Lily had witnessed a badly dressed, older gentleman entering the area. She said that he first appeared to talk to himself, before approaching a young woman named Leia.

"Leia is lovely. Popular with all the locals down here."

The detectives had yet to catch up with Leia, though Lily was clear that the exchange appeared to be completely innocent. The man then approached the shack.

"He mumbled a little. I couldn't really understand what he was saying. He was talking about something to do with stars though.".

He then took a seat on a bench near the area where the children played. Lily thought this a little odd so continued to watch.

"A couple of parents called their kiddies back and took them off."

After a while though it seemed to Lily that people had stopped noticing the old man's presence.

"He sat there for a good long while. Then he got up and started to work his way around the other benches."

He apparently was sitting next to people and looking to engage them in conversation.

"Each time he sat next to someone they got up and left pretty soon after."

At the end of her shift Lily locked up the shack then noticed that the old man had dozed off. "I looked about and could see that there were still plenty of people here, so I decided not to worry about it, you know. I figured that someone would wake him up before it got too late."

At this point Lily then left the scene.

The next people that the detectives spoke with were a well-known gang of youths, mostly black and Asian, that liked to hang out in the park after dark. They reported that they had first come across an old man on the bench near the children's play area. The leader of the gang, a young man named Joseph, stated.

"We seen him sleeping there and it was like already dark, you know. So, we thought we best wake him up like. We didn't wanna see no old dude dying of the cold."

They reported him as being scared and confused when he awoke, so they spent some time talking and interacting with him to try and make him feel more comfortable.

"We were all having fun. The old guy seemed alright you know. Then suddenly he got all confused and angry. Started throwing his arms about the place, shouting 'boom' over and over."

The group eventually concluded that the old man must be homeless. He was obviously in need of some help.

"We decided to take him to the overnight shelter. You know the one just over the road." They stated how they had helped other homeless people in the park previously and had come to know the shelter manager quite well.

"Meant we were able to jump the queue like."

After arriving at the venue, they handed the man over to the shelter manager and left.

Orwell and Huxley had spoken with the shelter manager, Catherine Booth, who was on shift that night. Catherine recalled one of the group bringing the old man in.

"I remember Joseph being extra concerned about this one. The old man looked cold and pale and I remember he was shaking a lot."

Catherine took over his charge and led him into the warmth of the building.

"I sat him down and got him a hot cup of tea. I tried to make conversation with him, tried to get him to tell me his name, but it was no good. He just kept mumbling, saying he felt sick."

Half an hour later Catherine decided to show the man to a bed so that he could rest.

"It was late, and I figured a sleep would do him good. We could then figure out what to do in the morning."

Having made sure he had everything he needed for the night she left him and went back to work. That was the last time she saw him.

The final witness the detectives spoke with was a homeless man also staying at the shelter. Well known to the locals, the man's name was Jacob Morley. He was in the bed next to the one that have been offered to the old man

"Cathy asked me to help the new guy settle in. No bother to me. He was mumbling but drifted off pretty quick. Next thing I wake up and he is all like sobbing an shouting an stuff. Kept calling out for 'Ebony', whoever that is."

Jacob stated that then, at approximately a quarter to three, the man sat bolt upright in the bed. Swung out his feet and stood up. He pulled on his tattered coat and without a word he made for the exit. According to pathology, less than 30 minutes after that time the old man was dead.

Based on the distance from the shelter and the location of the dead man's body, Orwell and Huxley had been able to deduce that the old man had left the shelter and then headed straight back into the main body of the park. Clearly someone had spotted him, realised he was an easy target and followed him. Said person had somehow managed to get ahead of the old man and when he turned his final corner, back toward the children's play area, the attacker struck.

'VOOMP!'

A single knife blow to the chest. It was enough to take the old man straight down. After this the attacker grabbed his legs and dragged him into the small copse of trees. The attacker had then gone through the old man's pockets, relieved him of what possessions and identifying documents he might have had. The attacker then left the old man to die alone.

So, this is how it had actually ended for our hero, Charlie Thatcher. An old man, sick, tired, lost and alone. In a haze of confusion and mental illness Charlie's life ended, at the hands of a mindless thug. There was no hate nor malice involved, just some grubby business and bad luck.

The local press of course reported on the tragic murder of an old man in the local park. The local people, whilst reading the news articles, on their phones over their cornflakes, were of course outraged and disturbed at what they read. Some even managed to read the whole story before flicking onto the next or letting themselves be lured in by clickbait adverts and funny videos embedded within the page. The story took less than three days to stop generating clicks. For a lost old man there was no public outcry and the police... Well, the police had budgets to consider and more pressing crimes to investigate. The case was eventually shelved, the attacker never caught. Charlie's body was shipped to the morgue. When nobody came forward to claim the body it was hygienically dispatched.

No final resting place.

No fancy headstone.

No-one left to mourn the man that was Charlie Thatcher.

To them he did not become a star.

The Cosmos, consumed within its own dream, neither noticed nor cared, nor did any soul residing within it.

Except, maybe...

Epilogue 2

Remembered

*'If you remember me, then I don't
care if everyone else forgets'*
Haruki Murakami

Dear Charlie,

You won't remember me but I work in the fish n chip shop, that used to serve you when you came in for your chips each week. My name is Ella by the way. I am part Asian, and I am 17. I saw your story of what happened to you in the newspaper and my therapist suggested I write you this letter, even though I know you won't ever get to read it, apparently it will be good for me to write it.

I see a therapist because I have had some troubles fitting in with the world. You see I don't really fit, and never had. My mum was adopted. My dad left soon after I was born. I have no brothers or sisters and don't have any real friends. I've tried to fit in, but I always seem to be on the outside of everything looking in. When I was younger, I used to hurt myself. It sounds silly now, saying it out loud, but it used to help. It was something I was in control of you see. It was like causing physical pain acted as a focus for the feelings inside me. It was like being able to get them out of me and then watch them heal.

Anyway, it all got a bit regular, and my mum decided to send me to see someone, which is why I am seeing a therapist and writing you this letter now. The job at the chip shop was their idea too. Well, not the chip shop, just any job really, but it just so happened there was where was hiring, They were right too. It has helped. When it's really busy I don't think of anything else other than getting them chips wrapped, and it's nice to know I am helping people. Without me some of them would go without their tea and have to be hungry.

Anyway, that is why I am writing you this letter, because I need to say thank you. When I started at the chip shop on my first ever day, I felt so scared and so sick and I wanted to run away and go and hurt myself. Then you walked in and I seen your eyes and I knew somehow that you would know what I was feeling and that in some ways somehow you felt the same things.

You came to the counter and gave me this kind smile. I remember you smelled a bit funny but somehow that didn't matter, not even a little bit. Your kindness that day made me feel stronger and I decided that if you could stick it then so could I. I looked forward to the next time you would come in after that and then I looked forward to seeing you each week, hoping you would notice the progress I was making.

I always wanted to chat to you, to ask you your name. I wanted to hear about your life and find out what your story was. I could never get the courage up to ask though and now it's too late. That is why my therapist said to write you this letter. I don't even know where they put you so I don't know yet where to take it, but I know I will find a place where you can see it.

I kept a coin you gave me as well. I always intended to tell you, to give it back. That first time you bought chips, I noticed in the money you gave me was a rare 50p. It's one with clouds on the back. I swapped it for one in my pocket and intended to give it back to you to tell you how valuable it was. Looks like I will need to look after it now though. One day maybe I can pass it on to someone else.

Anyway, I haven't quite got it all figured out yet, but I think I am getting there now. Thanks to my therapist (who actually looks a little bit like a monkey by the way :-) And thanks to you. I am thinking about studying now, to become a doctor maybe, or something like that where I can help other people. People like you maybe.

I wanted to write you something special just for you. I like to write poems, not that they're any good mind, but it seems to help get my feelings out. My therapist helped me a little with this one though - which is especially for you for helping me. I hope you like it.

> *I took a little time out to ponder*
> *A quiet moment to reflect*
> *I realised that I was tired already*
> *Of whatever it was that was to come next*
> *But in that same moment of ponder*
> *I come to realise how*
> *It's not what's next that matters*
> *All that matters is, here and right, now*

Thank you for being in the world Charlie Thatcher and thank you for helping me.
You will be remembered.

Love
Ella Songg
The Girl from the Chip Shop

Acknowledgments

So, to the acknowledgements. Surely the hardest part of any book to write. Fraught only with danger for the writer I feel. I mean, if anyone reads the book in the first place, nobody really goes on to read the acknowledgements. Unless of course they know the writer and are expecting to find their name in this section.

Danger 1 - Accidental Omission.

Assuming that the early onset has not been an issue, and the writer manages to mention everyone that deserves to be mentioned, they may then find that some of said persons didn't enjoy the book or found parts of it offensive etc, and, in this scenario, would much rather their name were not mentioned.

Danger 2 – Unsolicited Inclusion.

Finally, reeling off a long list of names (to avoid danger 1) might be interpreted as the writer trying to give the impression that they are super popular, have a gazillion friends and acquaintances, and is guaranteed the readership of them all.

Danger 3 – Accidental Ego.

Regarding this third danger at least, most of my friends don't even read books so, apart from the hippy, it's would likely be a complete waste of time offering them any thanks anyway. All that said, I do of course need to acknowledge some key people. So here goes...

Firstly, my incredible wife (aka carer), Andrea Cook/Watts. Andrea has had to listen to me whittle on about Charlie and clouds for a fair few year now and has somehow always managed to remain encouraging. Ebony is not based on you, but you are my Ebony and I thank you.

Me dad, Peter Cook. He definitely won't read this book (will be more interested in his fish cake and chips). It matters not. He is probably the best storyteller the world will never know, but I do. He kind of introduced me to the idea of Charlie and, whilst I wish things were different, I am grateful for that.

Me mam, Karen Drinan. who I know definitely will read this book. More than anything I thank you for not letting me forget about the Monkeys & Dragons :-)

Special acknowledgment goes to some of the founding members of Sunday Drink Club (sadly now defunct - so I think I'm allowed to talk about it). Jodie, Jamie, Whizz & Evie – original creators of Lord

Gangles, whom I at once fell in love with, adopted and adapted as my own.

A nod also to my uncle, Paul Johnson. He has written his own book, and in doing so helped inspire me to push on with mine. More recently he helped prepare me for the traumas of first-time self-publication and he was right, it is a minefield.

Okay, I could go on but, as already said, nobody is really that interested. Just to be on the safe side though I offer my acknowledgment and thanks to all the souls I know, all the souls I've ever known, and all the souls I've yet to meet. I care about you all more than you could ever know. Well, there is maybe one person out there I couldn't give a stuff about but, in the main, I love you and thank you all. Peace.

Oh, as a final point, the scene in 'Commerce', with Laissez-Faire and the circulating 10 Euro. Just need to be clear that is not an original idea. I read this on the internet, where a student of someone proposed the dilemma. I decided to include a version of it here. Also, Sid's teachings (Virtue) are of course The Buddha's teachings (albeit as I have interpreted).

Everything else though has fell out of my own head. Sorry xx lol :-)

Printed in Great Britain
by Amazon